Witches, Werewolves And Walter
By
Larry L. Deibert

1

Acknowledgements

The author would like to thank his staff of editors. Without your expertise, I could not have offered the reader as fine of a book as you have helped to make it. Thanks, Linda Berghold, Nick Zumas, Edward Gibney, and my wife, Peggy Deibert.

I would like to thank the people who have appeared in this book as themselves: Steve and Mary Wright, owners of the fabulous Carolina Temple Island Inn, in Wrightsville Beach, North Carolina. I would also like to thank their daughter, Rachel Wright Gilbert and her daughter, Molly Gilbert for appearing.

Thanks to my number one fan, Sherrl Wilhide, for her appearance.

I would like to show my appreciation to   Steve Harris for imparting his knowledge of drones to me.

Thanks to my beta readers, Ann Labe, Anita Gogno, Jack Hillman, Sherry Kromer, and Fred Scholl for their input.

Thank you, Alaska Angelini for creating a wonderful cover for this book.

I also want to thank God for giving me this gift of storytelling. Any religious mistakes I may have made are mine alone. My intent was to create a story full of possibilities and I truly regret any errors.

Before

Although *Witches, Werewolves and Walter* is a stand-alone novel, a number of characters, places, and actions from my five previous paranormal works have found their way into this book. In order to minimize any confusion you may refer to the list of characters at the end of the book.

In *The Christmas City Vampire,* set mainly in Bethlehem, Pa., between Black Friday and Christmas Day, 2010, a vampire must slay five beautiful, young women in order to end a one hundred and fifty year curse.

Hyram Lasky, a Bethlehem detective, is the lead investigator. Mike McGinnis, a patrol officer, is the first on the scene when the first victim is killed.

Werewolves In The Christmas City takes place in Bethlehem five years later. A Lehigh University student is slain in a harvested corn field, and once again, McGinnis is the first on the scene. A resident witnessed the murder and is positive that the victim was ripped apart by a werewolf. Lasky interviews her and prepares for another reign of terror.

A secret government facility is found and it is there that werewolf clones are being created. Two of the clones, Adam and Eve, return to human form, but still have certain powers; however they are unable to turn back into werewolves. They escape to Wilmington, North Carolina, where they take new identities. They are accompanied by a young man, Jamal Washington, who was scratched by a werewolf, and now has incredible powers.

Susan Mitchell, a reporter for the Saucon Valley Press is the first person outside of a small circle of police and others who learn about the werewolves.

Mike McGinnis's partner, Nikki Lawson, also joins in the fight.

Sherrl Wilhide, a waitress at the Brass Rail Restaurant in Allentown, Bethlehem's bordering city, is the first civilian to slay a werewolf, and her life will never be the same.

In *Fathoms,* the story begins seventy years after a sailor disappears aboard the battleship North Carolina during the battle of the Marianas Islands in 1944. His widow, his grandson and his wife, several of his long-dead shipmates, a blind attorney, Rick Conlen and his girlfriend Denise Scott, help solve the mystery of the sailor's disappearance. A number of other interesting characters find their way into this book.

From Darkness To Light introduces God, in the guise of a George Burns lookalike, because God loved the movie, *Oh God.* Mr. Burns portrayed God in the movie and our creator thought that was wonderful. God is assisted by a ten year old angel, Hannah, as they assemble a team of ghost hunters to send all earthbound spirits to their final reward, be it heaven or hell. The hunters come from all across the country, and each one had a physical malady, or a paranormal experience to bring them together to battle the spirits.

Family is a novel of immortality that spans 226 years. Julian Ross, the world's only immortal gives the gift to six humans and a three-legged dog named Riley. Graeme McDougal and Riley became immortal in 1793 and they were friends of the witch named Lucinda.

I've always wanted to write about witches, but did not have enough in mind for a novel, or even a short story. I decided to satisfy myself by adding them to this book.

I hope that this introduction will give you enough information about characters, places and actions to help power you through the book.

Hyram, Susan And Sherrl

Wrightsville Beach, North Carolina
July 10th, 2016

1

Hyram Lasky's sneakers pounded the macadam with each stride he took. On the final mile of his five mile run, he was enjoying the warmth of the early morning sun, and the breeze coming inland from the Atlantic Ocean. His chest burned as he ran faster and faster, sucking in oxygen and expelling the carbon dioxide from his lungs. At sixty-three, he really felt good, even with three prosthetic limbs. He lost both legs below the knees and his right arm below the elbow. It took him quite a while to adjust to the new limbs, but he never gave up.

With about a quarter mile to go to the Carolina Temple Island Inn, he started walking to cool down a little. He turned his face toward the Banks Channel of the Intracostal Waterway, watching boats cruise up and down. Taking the water bottle from the back left pocket of his shorts, he took a long pull, emptying the twenty ounce bottle. He put the container back in his pocket, then he wiped his brow with his left arm. The run was exhilarating, with no pain at all, finally feeling totally accustomed to the artificial limbs. Every day since January 31st, he thanked God for sparing his life. Six of his friends and co-workers were not as lucky and they died horribly after the bombs went off.

Lasky stepped onto the gravel parking lot, noticing a vintage Bentley automobile that had not been parked there when he left for his run. He strolled over and took a good look at it. The black car shone brightly and the interior was immaculate. White side walls gleamed on each tire. After strolling completely around the vehicle, he headed to the porch where he saw a portly man, sporting a white beard, wearing shorts, and a t-shirt, sweeping the side of the wraparound wooden porch. He was finally going to meet the owner of the Inn, Steve Wright.

2

Steve heard sneakers crunching on the gravel and looked toward the sound, where he saw Hyram Lasky walking toward the porch. Out of the corner of his eye he saw his wife, Mary, and their other special guest, Susan Mitchell, coming down the stairs from the second floor apartments. When he first met Susan about an hour ago, he was impressed by the woman with one arm. He knew that Hyram and Susan both lost limbs when the restaurant they were in, celebrating Lasky's retirement, was engulfed in a maelstrom of fire, smoke and debris after three bombs exploded, killing six and injuring seventeen. Steve's friend, Ed Gibney, wanted to pay for a vacation for the two survivors, but after Steve read Susan's report of the werewolves in the Christmas City, he chose to have them come down as his guests, instead.

Hyram Lasky stepped up on the porch and kissed Susan; then he turned to Steve. "Mr. Wright, it is such a pleasure to meet you and to thank you for giving Susan and me your apartment for a week. It is gorgeous." He shook Steve's hand.

"No, Mr. Lasky, the pleasure is all mine and please call me Steve."

"I like being on a first name basis with everyone, Steve. Call me Hyram or Hy."

"You appear to be getting around really well on those pegs of yours. Did it take long to get accustomed to them?"

Hy laughed at the word pegs. "Yeah it took a long time, but now I can pretty much do anything, and I really love to run. When I was still a detective, I was eating poorly and got myself noticeably out of shape. One time a friend saw me running and yelled to me, 'At least you run faster than a speeding building, although almost imperceptibly" I hoped someday to prove him wrong, but I never thought I'd have to lose both legs to do it. I guess after learning how to eat right and exercising, I should have a good, long life. Susan and I were fortunate to walk away from the carnage that day."

"Susan was just telling me everything that happened to you two; I am truly amazed with the fact that you both survived." Mary said. "I asked her and now, Hy, I'm asking you if you would mind telling the story to our guests tonight on the front porch? I'd also like to invite Seth McGuire, a reporter with the Wrightsville Gazette to write a story about you both. How do you feel about that, Hy?"

He looked at Susan, who nodded slightly, and answered, "Of course, Mary. We'd love to talk with him. Now, I'd like you to answer a question. I'm starving, and I am looking for a good breakfast. Where should we go?"

She replied, "On the other side of the bridge to your left is the Causeway Café. They have the best shrimp and grits I ever ate, along with any breakfast item you can think of. Get an order of their green fried tomatoes, too I guarantee you will love them."

"Thanks, that sounds great." Turning toward Susan, he said, "I'm going to take a quick shower and then we can head out. There's a lot of shopping for you to sink your teeth into."

He said to Steve and Mary, "What time should we be back?"

"We usually begin our cocktail time around 5 PM, and I think we will be going rather late this evening. We'll have some snacks and drinks for you guys."

"Great. By the way, who owns the Bentley?"

"A very good friend of ours, Laurence Hastings. That would be Laurence with a u. He is a retired professor of literature and he has been coming here for about forty years. He lost his wife a couple of years ago and rarely comes out on the porch for cocktails, but when I told him about you guys, he relished the thought of meeting you and Susan. Is your friend coming later?"

"Yeah, Sherrl Wilhide will be here probably around cocktail time. She's looking forward to meeting you and Mary."

"Laurence is looking forward to meeting her, too. She is the only civilian to ever kill a werewolf and I'm sure she'll put us all on the edge of our seats with that story."

"Okay, Steve. We'll see you guys about five. What can we bring to the soirée?"

Steve laughed. "Laurence will love that word. He always tries to have the best word of the day; however, I got him last night with the work crepuscular."

Hy cocked his head, and shrugged his shoulders.

"It means occurring or active in twilight hours. I learned it when I was studying to be a marine biologist."

"That must be messy, cutting those Marines apart?" Hy laughed at his own joke.

"Good one, Hy. I think you and Laurence will get along quite well."

As Hy bounded up the stairs, he said, "See you later."

Steve watched him fly up the stairs and turned to Susan. "He really moves well on his prosthetics. How is he mentally?"

"He's actually doing well inside his skin and head. Once in a while we both have nightmares but since we shared the same trauma, it is easy for us to talk about what is bothering us at any given time. He has a great deal of hatred for those who did this to us, and this could be a problem as time goes on. All I know is I love him and I want both of us to have a good, happy life. You folks have given us a great start with this vacation and I can't thank you enough."

3

After a great day of breakfast, shopping, lunch, more shopping, and then getting groceries at the local Harris Teeter, Hy and Susan returned to the Inn and lugged all their packages upstairs to the Wrights' apartment. They put everything in its place and then took hot showers. They had about an hour to kill until cocktail time, so they strolled out to the porch and sat in rocking chairs, enjoying the afternoon sun, and a light breeze. Boats of all sizes were heading up and down the channel. About a half dozen people were at the dock, fishing and swimming A fire was burning in one of the grills, flames rising above the grate, and they caught a whiff or two of burgers cooking. The smells were making them hungry and they were looking forward to snacks and drinks.

Susan had bought a pre-made tray of meats and cheeses and one of crackers. Hy had bought a case of Dos Equis for everyone to share. They both thought the evening would be a lot of fun, even with having to share their trauma with strangers. They just felt so comfortable and were sure the night would go well.

At 4:30, Hy and Susan lifted themselves from the comfy rockers and went inside to grab the snacks and beers for the porch party. Earlier, Susan had walked around the first floor perimeter and after arriving on the front porch she noticed a sign above a two-person swing that read *What Happens On The Porch Stays On The Porch.* She smiled when she read that. They left the wonderful air-conditioning of the apartment, and headed down the stairs to the porch.

4

They stepped on the porch to the applause of many people, both on the porch, or standing on the street in front of the Inn. Shocked, not knowing exactly how to respond, they both simply nodded and Steve asked them to sit on the swing, so everyone could see them and they could see everyone.

Steve introduced all who were on the porch. There was a young born again Christian couple from Ohio, their two toddlers sitting on the floor; a mother and daughter from Pittsburgh were seated on the small love seat. Sitting on the hammock, side by side, were two gay women from Kentucky. A young, aspiring novelist from Colorado was smoking a cigarette and sitting on the railing. A middle-aged couple from Florida, carrying a violin and a guitar, stepped up onto the porch from the street. Two young couples, who had arrived on their boat from Georgia, relaxed on rocking chairs. Laurence sat on a comfortable wicker chair. This was his forty-third consecutive year vacationing at the CTA-short for Carolina Temple Apartments. Seth McGuire, the reporter from the Wrightsville Gazette, sat on the floor by the rear steps, camera in hand, taking picture after picture. After the introductions concluded, Steve said, "Our other guests were not able make it to cocktail hour because of prior commitments, but they are hoping to return before we break up for the night."

He then introduced his special guests. "Hyram Lasky is a retired Bethlehem, Pennsylvania Police Department detective and Susan Mitchell is a reporter for the Saucon Valley Press. Unless you have been living under a rock, I'm sure you followed the story of the werewolves in the Christmas City. Bethlehem has been designated as such for many years. Six years ago, Hyram was the lead detective who helped destroy the Christmas City vampire. As you can see, they have both suffered greatly from a bombing that took place on January 31st. Over sixty friends and co-workers were gathered in a restaurant, celebrating Hyram's retirement, when numerous explosive devices were triggered, killing six and injuring seventeen. Hyram and Susan have offered to tell you all about that night, and then they'll answer questions. Before they begin, I suggest you refresh your drinks, grab a plate of food and then sit back and strap in. I think we're going to be taken on a hell of a ride by these two."

Bethlehem, Pennsylvania
January 31st 2016

1

Hyram Lasky finished clearing his office of his personal effects, and a couple of cops helped him put everything in his car. He came back inside and shook hands with his fellow officers who would not be able to make it to the bar for his retirement party tonight. He was given hugs, handshakes, congratulatory remarks, and a card signed by everyone on duty that night. He also received an unexpected and surprisingly hefty check as a parting gift. He was choked up after he walked from the building and opened the card. The check was in the amount of $2400 and he had to stop, catch his breath, and wipe some tears from his eyes.

He drove home, brought his gifts and memorabilia inside the house, and then went upstairs to take a shower. The hot water soothed him. He finished, dried off, and dressed in casual clothes, looking forward to having some good food and copious drinks. He decided to take Uber to and from the bar.

When the driver picked him up, he kept looking out the window, seeing people still cleaning up from Snowmageddon, as some were calling the blizzard. Bethlehem had received thirty-one inches of snow over a two day period a week ago. Hyram had a bunch of neighborhood kids take care of his snow removal for $100. There was no way he was going to break his back when there were youngsters willing to do the job and make a few bucks. The four teenagers were very happy with the money he gave them.

The driver dropped him at the bar, packed with off-duty cops and civilian well-wishers; his arrival elicited a long round of applause. He took his seat directly in front of the large window facing the street.

After a couple rounds of drinks, two cops excused themselves to go to the bathroom. That was what saved their lives.

Moments later, explosive devices were triggered. Earlier, they had been placed under each table where the guests were seated. The explosions rocked the building, shards of wood, metal, and glass flying throughout the bar.

When the dust settled, six people were dead and seventeen patrons were injured. Hyram Lasky survived, but his legs and right arm were gone.

He was dazed, not even realizing the extent of his wounds until he looked at himself, seeing three stumps where his legs and arm used to be. He vomited and then the pain hit him in waves. He howled in anguish, but when he heard the cries of many others, he pulled himself together and gritted his teeth. Susan Mitchell was lying on the floor beside him. She appeared to be unconscious and he saw her right arm was gone several inches below the elbow.

There were bodies everywhere and the cries of the wounded were chilling to hear. Some people were walking around, holding bloody napkins in their hands, trying to stem the flow from superficial wounds. A Bethlehem police officer, Harold Jenkins, was trying to remove a large splinter of glass from his stomach; blood was squirting everywhere and Lasky was afraid that if Hal removed the glass, he would bleed to death quickly. He saw another officer, Mickey Patterson, a former army medic, race to Hal to work on his wound.

2

Susan Mitchell was coming around. Although she was unable to open her eyes because they were covered with drying blood from other people; she was able to hear the pandemonium throughout the restaurant. People were screaming, but she could hear voices of reason trying to calm the injured. She still wasn't sure what had happened, but she felt herself being thrown from her chair and she felt the pain in her arm, seeing it separate below the elbow. All she could think of was that it would be easier learning how to use a below the elbow prosthetic then an above the elbow one. When she hit the floor, she looked for Hyram, hoping he would be okay, but a body fell on her and knocked her out.

She felt someone tie a tourniquet around her severed arm and then the person wiped the blood from her eyes and sat her up against a wall. He smiled at her and then moved on to another injured person. She saw he was an EMT and was thankful that professional help had arrived.

Seeing clearly now, she looked around and was sickened by the scents of burning flesh, spilled blood and guts, and copper wires burning. The sprinkler system became activated and everyone was getting soaked. Susan wretched when she saw one of their waitresses impaled by a steel pipe; her body hanging from a wall.

Hearing his voice next to her, she reached out for Hyram. She found his left hand, squeezed it and felt him squeeze back. She prayed that they were both going to be okay.

3

Mike McGinnis was in the men's room when the explosions went off. He quickly zipped up and took a pistol from the ankle holster under his slacks. He cautiously opened the door, and stepped into a pool of blood. He looked down and saw the body of a cop that he knew slightly. His throat was severed by a piece of a table or chair and he must have died covering the wound with his hands, attempting to stop the bleeding. Mike gulped back some bile, and moved past the body, searching for the living.

His partner, Nikki Lawson, who had also taken a bathroom break, heard three explosions as she was sitting on the toilet. She got up and quickly pulled up her jeans. She drew a handgun from her purse and exited the bathroom, looking for targets. Seeing no danger from anyone in the restaurant, she put the weapon back in her bag. She saw that the three tables reserved for the party were blasted to pieces. Apparently, the explosives must have been attached to the bottoms of the heavy wooden tables. *Was someone who works here responsible for this act or was it someone who had known about the party and placed the devices in advance?* Nikki needed to tell Mike her suspicions, but first she had to see if anyone needed help.

Mike was talking to Hy when he saw Nikki looking around at the damage. He caught her eye and waved her over.

She saw Hy and Susan and muttered, "Oh my God!" A moment later, she was crying, but Hy stroked her cheek to try to comfort her.

"Nikki, Susan and I are going to be alright. How many have died today?"

Mike told him who perished and Hy was in total disbelief. "Are you absolutely certain, Mike?"

"Yes, Hy. I'm so sorry."

Although nobody seemed to know how the paramedics arrived so soon after the explosions, they were busy trying to save lives. Two stretchers were brought over and Mike and Nikki helped place Hy and Susan on them. They were wheeled out to a waiting ambulance which was soon on its way to Lehigh Valley Hospital, sirens wailing furiously.

Wrightsville Beach, North Carolina
July 10th, 2016
Continued

5

You truly could have heard a pin drop as each person was in rapt attention, clinging to every word that Hy and Susan spoke. Even the kids managed to keep silent, somehow knowing that what was being said and listened to was very important; too important to be interrupted. The girl, Christina, understood a little more because she was two years older than her brother, Max, now fast asleep on the blanket on the floor. She stared at everyone on the porch and saw sad faces; even her mom and dad were wiping tears from their eyes.

Their parents, Hal and Stephanie Ormond, were concerned that the talk of vampires and werewolves would frighten the kids and they were prepared to take their children off the porch if they got scared.

When she heard Mr. Lasky talking again, she turned toward him.

"The pain was becoming unbearable, but the paramedics gave me something to ease it as we sped toward the hospital. I could feel every bump we hit on the way, but that was nothing compared to the mental anguish I was beginning to feel. Seconds before the explosion, I was a carefree, brand new retiree with a good pension, a nice nest egg in investments, and cash on hand, looking forward to the many things I planned to do, and now, a moment later, I was missing both legs and an arm. Obviously, I discerned that I would be able to do many things someday, but I'd have to go through a gruesome recovery to get there. The one thing I had going in my favor is that I am a patient man. I think that is one of the good things I learned during all those years of police work." He chuckled a little. "Watching cop shows on TV always makes me laugh because cases are solved in record time." He picked up his beer and took a healthy pull, allowing Susan to jump in and talk.

"I have a lot of respect for Hy because I don't know if I could endure having both legs gone. I have been able to deal with my prosthetic arm but I really miss having my own hand and fingers, sometimes..."

Christina jumped up and said, "Can you show us how your fake arm and hand works? They look pretty cool, Miss Mitchell."

Susan and Hy both laughed. It was always amazing how children could break the tension. The others on the porch also began to laugh and the noise woke Max. He sat up and rubbed his eyes.

"Bubba" Christina said, using his nickname, "Miss Mitchell is going to show us how her arm and hand works."

Max got up and nonchalantly eased his way over to her, wanting to get a closer look.

Susan tousled his hair with her prosthetic hand and then showed him, and everyone, how she worked it. First she took it off and Max got big eyes, seeing her stump. "Can I touch it, Miss Mitchell?"

"Of course you may, and please call me Susan." She looked at Christina and said, "Do you want to touch my arm, too?"

Christina was by her side in a shot, rubbing her stump. "Your skin is so smooth, Susan."

"Yes, it is. I have to keep my skin soft and pliable so I don't get any sores." Susan fit the prosthetic over her arm and tightened it above her elbow. Although she was focusing on Christina and Max, everyone was fascinated watching her. "I press sensors on the arm to change its position and the muscles in my upper arm actually help control the way my hand moves." She took her left hand and changed the position of her prosthetic thumb. "I can make a fist, open and close my hand, and this is the one that really freaks people out when they are watching me closely and I am in a playful mood." She opened her hand fully and then curled each finger back toward her palm. She moved her pointer finger back and forth in a come here motion and she looked at the faces of everyone, seeing a wide range of emotions, from shock to total delight. The kids started clapping and the adults also joined in. Several passersby had stopped and stepped up onto the porch to watch the demonstration, too.

It seemed like Hy and Susan were bombarded with a million questions, but they answered every one as best as they could. They continued to enjoy snacks and beverages, and Hy began to feel a little tipsy, but he was on vacation and could sleep it off in the morning. As he took a sip of beer, a young woman, one of the boaters, inquired, "You said that six people died that day and I just wondered if you could tell me about them."

Hy said nothing for several moments and then nodded. "We lost two police officers, two of the waitresses serving us and two that really hit me hard. My friend, Everett Gardner, who was the local coroner, was found dead. A large piece of the window, or something else made of glass, pierced his throat and he must have struggled before he died." He stopped and wiped some tears from his face. "Just after we were loaded on to stretchers, I saw Nikki. I think she was looking for her husband, Chuck. I didn't know he had died until she visited me in the hospital and told me he was killed by blunt force trauma by some items that flew through the air from the explosion. She was devastated, but she is doing pretty well now."

6

Moments later, a diminutive women came around the corner of the porch and yelled out, "Hi, y'all." She had spiked hair and was wearing John Lennon sunglasses, bright green flip-flops, a blue tank top that read 'Arkansas Is For Lovers' and multi-colored LuLaRoe leggings. A huge smile covered her face. She waved to everyone as she edged her way to the swing to stand beside Hy and Susan. Her entrance made them laugh until they almost cried.

Hy said, "Ladies, gentlemen, and kids, it is my pleasure to introduce Sherrl Wilhide, waitress extraordinaire, and werewolf slayer."

She curtsied to a round of applause and then took off her sunglasses to see everyone better.

Sherrl sat cross-legged on the floor in front of Hy and Susan on the swing. She took a sip of wine and was ready to speak when a squirrel jumped on her left thigh. "Who do we have here?" she asked, looking directly at Steve.

"That is Fred. He has been hanging around here since last year and we feed him peanuts. He has also invaded our morning coffee time, looking for treats. I guess he was interested in all the people here and will probably beg. I've never seen him hop up on someone, though. You must have some kind of mystical powers to have him do that."

"No, I don't think so," she laughed. "I guess Fred just likes me." She petted him and then began her story.

"Most of y'all read pretty much everything that was written about those couple of weeks in Bethlehem, so I'm not going to go into that too much, except to say it was a really frightening time. Don't think I was ever so scared, and I don't scare too easily.

"I was visiting my friend, Samantha, in Bethlehem; I live in Allentown which is a city that borders Bethlehem. She was afraid after hearing about the werewolves and asked me to come over to her house. Sometimes I wish she would have come to my house instead, but I believe God had other plans for me, so I traveled to her house. I brought some Brass Rail steak sandwiches and fries to warm up and eat by the fireplace as we watched TV and had lots of girl-talk.

"Sam got a phone call and left the room to talk, so I strolled out to the dining room to get the second half of my cheesesteak and some more fries, when I saw the TV screen change to a special report about werewolves busting loose from a secret facility in the mountain. Sam's house was in a nice development about a hundred yards from the base of the mountain, and I was hoping that the facility was at some other part of the mountain, but I was wrong.

"When Sam came back, I told her about the report I just saw on TV and we both wondered what we should do. We considered hiding, but I didn't think that would do anything more than trap us. We decided to turn off the lights and just stay put, hoping that if no light was seen from outside, the wolves wouldn't be attracted to her house."

Bubba came over and sat on Sherri's lap, not really understanding what was going on, but somehow knowing that she needed a friend right now. Sherrl ruffled his hair and kissed him on the forehead as Fred scampered to a corner of the porch and continued to wait to be fed.

"Sam went to turn off all the inside lights, and I walked to the front door to turn off the porch light. I was ready to flip the switch when I saw a shadow pass in front of the glass. I turned off the light and saw nothing, so I strolled back to the living room, but I felt as though I was being watched. Then I heard noise.

"The wolf crashed through the large front window, growling and spitting saliva, heading right toward me. Sam saw the beast and screamed loud enough that the neighbor across the street heard her. He had just stepped outside for a smoke. Adrenaline coursed through me as I turned toward the creature and quickly dove to the floor as the werewolf leaped over where I had just stood. I wound up in front of the fireplace, feeling the heat thrown off by the burning logs. I grabbed the silver tipped poker and the silver shovel as well.

"The wolf had leaped so far that it crashed into the dining room table, causing wine glasses and plates to fly. The table splintered when the animal hit it with all its force and that was just enough to stop its momentum, offering me the precious seconds I needed to prepare for a life and death fight. I was praying harder than I had ever prayed before and when the wolf got back on its feet, turning toward Sam who was cowering in a corner of the large room. I knew it was now or never. I charged the large animal, thrusting the point of the poker into its side as hard as I could and then I wielded the shovel like a sword and took a swipe at the wolf's neck, partially severing it from its body. The wolf howled in pain, its eyes now cloudy as I withdrew the poker from it and stabbed it where I thought its heart would be. Long moments passed as the wolf writhed and howled, finally falling to the floor in a pool of blood, dead.

"The adrenaline was beginning to wear off and I collapsed in a heap, while Sam raced to my aid.

"Several neighbors, who heard the howling and screaming, were now gathered just inside the door, staring at the gruesome scene with their mouths wide open. Two or three had the presence of mind to call 911. The cops had also been alerted by all the dogs in the neighborhood who were barking and howling.

"Within a few minutes, three patrol cars arrived at Sam's house. Three cops worked on crowd control and interviews with bystanders, while the other three went inside. The scent of a dead animal permeated the air, and even though the front door was no longer there, the cold air filling the house didn't lessen the odor very much. The cops were pretty much in disbelief when they saw the carcass of a wolf, probably nine to ten feet in length, lying on the floor. None of them had ever seen a wolf so large. The three were hunters and had seen a few on their hunts in Canada.

"They questioned us and waited for a detective to show up. That's the first time I met Hy and we've been friends since that horrible day.'

A dead silence ensued for a couple of minutes until Steve said, "Okay folks, we have lots of food and drinks, so let's have at it and give our speakers a little time to recoup." He had seen that the trio from Pennsylvania were crying and holding on to one another.

7

Hy and Susan stood up and ambled to the side porch where a table, still filled with food, was being attacked by many hungry souls. There was a cooler filled with beer, soda and water, and several wine bottles stood sentinel on another table with a filled ice bucket in the middle and plenty of plastic cups.

They all took their seats again and talked about what a great place they were staying at, complimenting Steve and

Mary until their hosts nearly turned red from all the attention.

The party continued until well after dark, and then Hy asked for everyone's attention.

He said, "Folks, thanks for sharing your evening with us, but this old man has to get his butt to bed." He hugged Steve and Mary and, of course, everyone wanted a hug from him and Susan.

8

The porch was empty, except for Steve, who was cleaning up. He felt the back of his neck prickle and turned toward his left. He saw a spirit sitting on the hammock, one that he had seen before. The apparition waved to him and Steve waved back. It was an old friend, Walter Marchant, who passed almost two years ago.

Walter

Southport, North Carolina
July 16th, 2014

1

Walter Marchant sat on his bunk in his cell. Having been here for almost seventy-two hours was unsettling indeed. Two police officers, Laura Beck and Mike Solomon had arrested him at Eric's Grille, where he was having breakfast with his old army buddy, Lennie Beckham. They told him he had killed his wife, which he adamantly denied. Granted, he wasn't able to tell them where he was when she was brutally murdered, but he absolutely knew he could not have committed such a hideous crime.

2

The worst thing he had ever done in his life was to steal a carton of cigarettes when he was a kid. He paid for that dearly because the store owner didn't punish him or call the cops; he called the old man. When Walter saw his dad later that day, he figured he'd be grounded forever, but what his dad dished out as punishment was worse than solitary confinement in his room.

His father, Stanley, a steelworker, sat his young ass in a wooden chair in the middle of the kitchen. He then sauntered over to the bank of cabinets above the kitchen counter and reached to the back on the top shelf of his junk cabinet, coming out with a huge, green cigar. He strolled back to Walter and smiled, handing him the cigar and a lighter. "Son, I've been saving this cigar for such a situation.

You see, when I was a kid, about your age, I was caught smoking by my old man, and he did the exact same thing to me that I'm going to do with you. As I smoked that cigar, I promised myself that I would never smoke again and I didn't. Now I want to see if it works with you. So, light up, and enjoy this fine cigar."

Walter smoked the cigar as his dad worked on a crossword puzzle book. Stanley loved all kinds of puzzles, but crosswords were his favorite. He also enjoyed Zane Grey western novels. Each puff of the long, green cigar, nauseated Walter more and more, but because he was a stupid teenager, he just kept smoking, until the cigar was about an inch long. He stood up and took the smoldering stogie to his father, showing him that he smoked the whole thing.

Stanley looked up from his puzzle and then looked at the stub of the cigar. Without cracking a smile he said, "So, how did you like that, Son?"

"It was a little weak." He spotted his mother's Pall Malls on the table and asked, "Ok if I take one of Mom's cigarettes?"

Stanley hated that his wife, Emma, smoked but she had at least cut down to less than half a pack a day. In disgust, he went back to his crossword and said, "Suit yourself, Kid, but I don't want to hear it when you start hacking and wheezing like your mom does."

3

"Marchant, you have a visitor," Police Chief Harlan Sanders announced, opening the door of the cell.

Attorney Richard Rick Conlen stepped inside the cell and sat next to his client. He opened his briefcase and pulled out a legal pad, ready to take notes from this meeting. Walter's trial was scheduled for a week from yesterday, and there was still a lot to go over. He would have liked more privacy, but in a small town, the jails don't always have an interview room.

The formerly blind litigator, grabbed his phone and read a text message, responding very quickly. "Sorry, Walter, Denise wants me to meet her at Fishy Fishy for lunch."

"No problem, Rick. I sure as hell ain't going anywhere soon, so take all the time you need to get ready for this session." He watched Rick look over some papers. The man was a miracle to modern medicine. Sightless since the age of fourteen, when he fell, skiing, Rick regained his sight just last week. Most everyone in Southport figured it was a miracle. God wanted him to see again, and even Doctor Mayotte, his optometrist couldn't explain it in any other way. "How is Denise doing?"

"She's great, Walter. Life is really good right now, but we're not here to talk about me or Denise. We have to figure out how to convince a jury you are innocent. Blaming your wife's death on a witch is pretty hard to prove, but I'm going to give it my best shot. I don't think you committed the crime and that's what I am going with. Tell me about that night again, please."

4

Walter was three sheets to the wind when he left Loco Jo's, a bar at the northern part of Southport. When he walked to his car, he was taken by surprise by a woman whom he had never seen before. She held a cigarette in her hand and asked, "Do you have a light?" He flicked open his Zippo lighter and the spark turned into a yellow glow as she took a drag. She was looking into his eyes, and he, hers. He felt compelled to kiss her.

Later, as they sat quietly in his car, looking at the moonlight on the ocean, she wanted him then and there. She leaned over and kissed him again, but he resisted, saying, "No! You are a beautiful woman, but I am happily married."

She laughed. "Happily married, my ass. You've been beating her for years, every time you come home drunk, and yet Helen stays with you. I just don't understand her."

Taken aback, he stammered, "H-how do you know Helen? I've never seen you before."

"Oh, but Walter, darling, you have seen me before. In fact, you and I dated when we were in high school."

"That's impossible. You don't look a day over thirty and I am sixty-three!"

"Ha ha, that's a good one, Walt. If I would reveal my true age and looks, you would probably have a heart attack. Back then, I was Gail Weichert. Let's see if you remember, now."

He lit a cigarette and thought for a while. "Yes, I do remember you, but how can this be?"

"I'm a witch, and you're not going to like what I'm going to do now."

5

Rick listened carefully.

"That's all I remember. The next thing I knew was sitting at Eric's, having breakfast with Lennie. When she told me I used to beat Helen, my mind raced because I would never have done anything like that. I don't know how she could have said that. Granted I do drink too much from time to time, but Helen always understood that my PTSD got out of hand sometimes and I drank to forget the horrible things that I did during that war."

"Let's talk a little bit about Vietnam. You were an infantryman with the Gary Owen Task Force near Bien Hoa in 1972. What was your mission?"

Walter had the faraway look of a combat veteran come over his face, and he was quiet for a long time, occasionally wiping tears from his eyes. "Yeah, we were stationed at FSB Green…"

"FSB?"

"Sorry. That would be Fire Support Base, Rick. Even though most of the troops were gone by March, we still participated in active search and destroy missions around Bien Hoa. It was some gruesome, tiring, violent work and we killed a large number of enemy soldiers. I never was bothered by killing enemy soldiers at a distance, but the final enemy soldier I killed was face-to-face. He was so close I could smell the fish on his breath. It was dark as hell and I was on a listening post about fifty yards outside the wire. My buddy, Hank Ebert was sleeping while I was on watch. I could hear extraneous noises that didn't belong and I was pretty sure the gooks were going to try to overrun Green." He stood up and began pacing, his hands were shaking badly.

After regaining control of his nerves, Walter sat back down and continued "The noises were getting closer, so I clicked the radio handset twice to alert the men inside the firebase. Chances were good that some of the enemy soldiers heard the sound, but, for some reason, I felt that they didn't. I didn't want to wake Hank because he had a habit of yawning loudly when awakened, and that noise they would hear for sure

"I had my knife out, not wanting to make extra noise with a rifle, when I smelled his breath, right in front of me.

I sliced through the air in front of me with the knife and I felt it hit flesh: a moment later, my hand was covered with hot blood. I got lucky and cut his jugular. He had no time to make a sound before he died. I put my bloody hand over Hank's mouth as I shook him awake. We were both unbelievably alert and adrenaline was coursing through our bodies. To this day, I don't know how we were missed, but we could hear them crawling toward the perimeter and about five minutes later, everyone at the base opened up with the loudest cacophony of noise I ever heard. All kinds of weapons were being fired. Hank and I had to duck down in our hole because the bullets were whizzing by our Listening Post.

"The screams of the wounded and dying chilled me to the bone and the incredible noise of weapons fire, especially coming toward me, was very unnerving. The firing ended as quickly as it began and I said to Hank, "I think we're going to be okay, Buddy." He didn't answer, so I felt around for him and found him dead. I never heard the bullet hit his head. A couple of moments later, I felt the pain and touched my shoulder. A round had gone through me, and I thought a bone might have been broken or shattered.

"At daylight, I looked toward the base and saw many bodies in unconceivable poses. Men were coming from inside the wire, checking the bodies and, hopefully coming for us. I turned around and saw the NVA I killed. It was a woman! Her eyes were wide open and the slit in her neck was so large. She was a good-looking woman, perhaps in her late teens or early twenties and here she was lying in her own blood, dead. I didn't feel remorse for killing her for many years. Then my nightmares began and she has been with me since." He looked at Rick and shifted gears, "I didn't kill Helen, and I know I never beat her. What are we going to do?"

"I don't know right now, but I promised Helen I would defend you to the absolute best of my ability."

"How could she have told you to defend me if she is dead?"

"Walter, this might sound a little crazy to you, but Helen came to me about nine hours after you supposedly strangled her and dumped her body in a well near LaCosta's farm. I was hoping she might have come to you before she was pulled toward Masonboro Island for The Gathering, but that didn't happen."

"What is The Gathering? I don't understand any of this, Rick."

"Okay, here it is in a nutshell. I am a ghost whisperer. I was blind, but a miracle gave me my sight back. God has enlisted eight people, through miracles, to send all earthbound spirits to their final reward, be it heaven or hell, at Masonboro Island. He named it The Gathering." Rick stopped to let Walter digest this information.

"Helen came to me and told me how you killed her, and what you did with her body. She also told me that you drove to my office and rifled through some files, but you didn't leave with anything, and I don't know what you could have possibly been looking for. A few moments later, Officers Beck and Solomon entered my office and asked a bunch of questions. Helen decided to reappear and she told the three of us that you were at Eric's Grille and that is when you were arrested." He laughed. "I thought the cops were going to scream when they saw Helen."

"I can't account for all the hours prior to breakfast, but one of my neighbors, Lucy Yates saw me at about 5:30 that morning. I had awakened because my shoulder was aching."

6

After sitting quietly for a few minutes, running all that was said through his mind, he abruptly changed the subject, saying, "I never finished my story. The guys from the firebase found Hank and I. I was medevacked to a military hospital in Saigon and after they repaired my shoulder, I was sent home. My fighting was over." He let out a huge sigh and wiped tears from his eyes.

Anyway, that morning, I made a cup of coffee and stepped outside for the paper. Lucy was on her front porch, smoking a cigarette and I walked over to bum one. I had run out just before I went to bed, so I was Jonesing when I saw her light up. "Did you go out during the middle of the night, Walt?" she asked. I told her I was in bed all night, and she shrugged her shoulders. "I couldn't sleep and I looked out the window. I thought your car was gone, but I guess I was wrong." I had forgotten about that till just now, but please check with her, Rick."

"I will. Okay, Walt, I gotta go, but I'll try to get back later."

"Thanks for defending me, Rick. I know you don't have much to go on, but that's all I can think of right now."

After Rick left, Walter turned toward a sound and saw the witch standing in his cell, laughing.

The Good Witches

Martha's Vineyard, Massachusetts
July 7th, 2016, Morning

1

Lucinda Barone finished loading her car and took a last look at the ocean off the coast of Martha's Vineyard. She had lived here for many, many years, but it was time to find her sisters, and take them to Southport, North Carolina for their fourth one-hundred year anniversary of becoming witches. Every century the seven sisters had to return to the oldest oak tree in the town, from which they would withdraw the energy needed for another one-hundred years of magic power. Her sisters were spread out all over the east coast, but as the oldest witch, twenty-seven in human years, she had the ability to mentally seek them out and find them quickly.

The community she resided in consisted of over three-hundred gingerbread style homes, most built in the late 1800's. The Oak Bluffs section of the Vineyard was at one time a meeting place for Methodists who lived in tents. When it became a more permanent community, the tents were replaced with the gingerbread cottages. Painted in lavishly bright colors, and well-maintained by year-round residents and those who only vacationed here in the summer, the community has been a must-see part of a visit to Martha's Vineyard. As she drove toward the ferry dock to make the trip to Cape Cod, she stopped in front of one house that was vacant. Her old friend, Graeme McDougal had lived here since the latter part of the nineteenth century.

2

Immortals since 1793, he, with his three-legged dog, Riley by his side, regaled many visitors with what they thought were simply creative or made-up tales, but were true-life stories of them and their friend, Julian Ross, who saved him and Riley from dying when their boat broke apart in the Loch during a storm. Julian and his "Family' of seven immortals were being hunted down. Most of the family, including Graeme, were systematically executed. Had Lucinda been on the island that day, she possibly could have saved him. She knew that Julian, his wife, Petra and Riley survived the slaughter and were now living somewhere on the west coast. Although she never met Julian, she enjoyed the stories Graeme told her.

3

She had met Graeme about fifteen years ago as she walked through her new community. His flowers were just outstanding and she had to stop by to compliment him. She approached his house and when her feet hit the pavement just inside the small picket fence surrounding the yard, a small brown and white dog popped up on the porch and strolled out to meet her. She saw he only had three legs, yet he walked so normally which impressed her. He barked a couple of times and then sat down in front of her, cocking his head from side to side. She did keep dog treats with her and she saw he was sniffing her jeans pocket. She knelt down and gave him a biscuit and petted him vigorously.

"I see Riley has made friends with you, young lady. The dog will never be able to guard me when he is always begging." Graeme laughed. "I'm Graeme McDougal."

She stood up and put her hand out to the one-legged man in a kilt. "Hello, I'm Lucinda Barone and I just moved here. I saw your flowers and had to come in your yard to smell them; then Riley greeted me. I think I'm in love with him. How did you both lose legs?'

Graeme sensed that she was not human, but he wasn't sure what he wanted to tell her. "I don't like to talk about the accident, so I'm going to pass on that question right now. May I offer you a cold drink? I have water, iced tea and Guinness, plus I also have some good Irish whiskey."

She laughed. "You had me at Guinness. I would love one, please."

"Wonderful. Please come on the porch and find a rocking chair while I get our drinks."

That led to a beautiful friendship that lasted until he died. She was glad that Riley lived.

She and Graeme both had the ability to mass hypnotize, so that no one could ever figure out how long they lived there. She gazed at the house for a moment and then drove away.

New York City
July 7th Evening

1

When Eliese Conway came on stage, Lucinda gasped for breath. Her younger sister, by only a year, was the most beautiful of the sisters. Wearing a long wig that fell to the middle of her back, only made her look more ravishing. Eliese was an ugly duckling as a toddler and stayed that way until puberty arrived. The physical changes in her body and face were nothing less than remarkable, and for a long time, Lucinda was quite jealous of her.

She was portraying a goddess from a realm not of this earth. Around her black hair, she wore a silver band that held a silver emblem with beads covering her forehead to nearly between her eyes. Her thick eyelashes enhanced her large, hazel eyes. Her regal nose was an attention grabber above lips the color of burgundy wine. She wore a floor-length silk gown that ended above her generous breasts. The aqua color and a silver broach looked exquisite. She wore silver slippers on her dainty feet and silver rings on every finger. She began to sing her opening number and as she gazed into the audience she saw her sister, smiling at her. The sight of Lucinda was also very troubling, and her eyes and mouth turned downward for just a brief moment. She regained her composure and played her character as though she would never again take the stage.

After the play ended and the cast received a standing ovation, Lucinda slipped out of her seat and headed toward the dressing room to see Eliese for the first time in this century. It was always an agony when they all met, because everyone would have to drop what they were doing and go to Southport for a reawakening.

They had powers, but as the century waned, their magic lessened and had be regenerated at the Reawakening ceremony. Perhaps this one would be different and they would never have to go through this ever again.

2

Seraphina on Broadway was not too crowded, offering Lucinda and Eliese an opportunity to talk without having to speak too loudly. There were many things a mortal should not hear coming from their mouths.

"Eliese, you were amazing," Lucinda said, after they were seated and their drink orders taken. "I never knew you had such a powerful, beautiful, voice, and your costumes only enhanced your loveliness even more with every change."

"Thank you, Lucinda. I am saddened, though, because now that you are here, I fear that I will not be able to continue with the play. I have been seeking a role like this for such a long time, and I think the show could have a long run." She offered a sad smile. "I guess my understudy will be taking over very soon?" she asked, looking into her sister's eyes.

Lucinda nodded. "I am so very sorry, Eliese, but we have less than a week to track down Amanda and Janelle and then get to Southport for the ceremony."

Eliese appeared confused. "What about the triplets? Nothing happened to them, I hope?"

"The ceremony will only be with the four of us. Giselle, Marta and Bella have chosen to go over to the dark side of witchery and I no longer have any control over them. There is a possibility that we might see them, but I can't be positive. Now, I'd like to talk about you. What made you become an actress? It seems so far removed from the types of work you have done in the past."

Their meals arrived and since Eliese had not eaten since breakfast, the conversation came to a complete stop until she devoured half of her steak, baked potato and broccoli. She also drank two glasses of wine in that time period.

She placed her knife and fork on her plate and finished chewing the mouthful she was working on before daubing her mouth with a linen napkin and taking one more sip of wine.

"I've been working at a law firm, something I really love, as you well know. One of my co-workers had aspirations of being an actress for years, ever since she was a kid. About five years ago, she asked me to go with her to a cold reading for a part in a five-person play. There would be three men and two women. Stephanie read for the lead and she did well. I was sure she would get it. The director asked me if I would like to read for the part of the second woman and I accepted. We both got the parts and studied our lines together. I fell in love with the stage from that moment and I've been lucky to get a bunch of great parts. Getting the lead in *Goddess,* was the culmination of several years of hard work. I am depressed that I have to give it up, but our sisterhood is more important than anything else in the world to me."

Just a moment before Lucinda was going to respond, five women stopped by their table. One said, "Eliese, we saw the show and wanted to tell you that we thought you were amazing. In a couple of weeks two gals are going to have to leave our show and we were hoping you would read for one of the parts."

"Thanks, Allison, I think I will. I don't know how long my show will run, but if I have the opportunity, I'd love to give it a shot. Glad you ladies could stop by. Enjoy your dinner."

As they walked away, Lucinda asked, "What play do they want you to read for?"

"*Wicked,*" is the untold story of the witches of *The Wizard of Oz.*"

The two witches could not contain their laughter.

Charleston, South Carolina
July 9th, 2016

The temperature was a brutal 91 degrees with not even a hint of breeze when Lucinda and Eliese sauntered into Poogan's Porch on Queen Street. A refreshing blast of cool air offered a comfortable dining experience for sure.

Built in 1888, the former Victorian home and the neighborhood had changed by 1976, offering the conversion of the house to a restaurant. The owners had sold the home and moved, but a little, brown dog named Poogan was left behind. The dog thought the porch was his property because he was in the neighborhood for years, wandering from porch to porch, looking for a little love and perhaps a handout from the home owners. When the restaurant was created, Poogan assumed the role of official greeter when people stepped on to the porch. Poogan died in 1979, but the restaurant and the porch he lived on continued to honor him.

The brunch crowd was nearly overflowing and they had to wait outside until a table opened in Amanda's section. Lucinda asked the hostess not to mention that anyone was here to see her specifically. It was going to be a great surprise.

The sisters were seated and watched Amanda Tarioli as she raced around the room, taking orders, filling water glasses and returning with food from the kitchen. It only took a short period of time before she spotted them and rushed over to give them warm hugs.

"Oh, it is so good to see you both, even though I know my time here will now end." She received quizzical looks from some of her regular customers. One said, "Amanda, are you leaving us?"

41

"Yes, Betty. My sisters and I have an appointment we must keep and I will have to leave after this brunch..." She saw Lucinda nod and continued, "I'll take good care of you folks, just like I always have before I must leave."

"Will you be back after your appointment?" Betty inquired.

"Sadly, no. We have one more sister to find before our appointment, and once we are together again, we have a lot of family business we must finish and I think that will take several years."

After brunch ended, Amanda requested her final pay. After receiving it and saying goodbye to all the staff and owners, the three sisters left to get Amanda's belongings from her place. She was miserable, having to leave all her nice furnishings, but she would get new things after the Reawakening. She took some of her clothes, toiletries, along with a few sentimental items and packed them all in one small suitcase.

Wrightsville Beach, North Carolina
July 10th, 2016

1

Early the next morning, they parked on Waynick Boulevard in Wrightsville Beach and then walked to the beach. Because it was so early in the day, the long stretch of sand was fairly deserted. Black clouds were forming on the horizon, promising the possibility of rain, thunder, and lightning. Lucinda figured it would begin in less than two hours.

She saw a family setting up a tent, and was concerned it would not protect them from the storm. They would all perish when a bolt would strike the tent shortly after they all huddled inside. It would not be a pretty sight for the police that would investigate.

A young man and his wife, who must have been nine and a half months pregnant, strolled in the sand. The mother-to-be wore a black bikini, the top sporting fringes that draped her huge belly and it was almost impossible to see her bikini bottom because her stomach was so large. Lucinda hoped they would leave the beach soon and get to a hospital because the baby was going to be born in ninety-two minutes.

Three teenagers, two girls and a boy, were playing Frisbee and listening to music playing from a boom box resting on the sand. It was rap, and Lucinda hated that kind of music, so she played a little trick and turned the station to one playing sixties rock. The kids were stunned and one boy ran to the radio and turned it back to the rap station. A moment later, the sixties music was playing again and the boy saw the three witches standing just below the dune. He didn't know *how* he knew they were witches, but he bailed on his friends as fast as his legs could carry him.

Two anorexic women were applying suntan lotion to each other. Lucinda could see their ribs plainly and shook her head. She could never understand how humans could abuse their bodies by starving themselves, or in the other direction, gorging themselves until they could barely move.

They saw Janelle Landon a moment later.

She wore a lime green, skimpy bikini, flip-flops, and a white fedora, with a black hat band. Sporting Foster Grant sunglasses, she was dancing on the beach to the tunes that seemed to always play inside her head. She shimmied and shook, spun around, high-kicked, and did cartwheels, drawing the attention of several young men, sitting on a blanket drinking beer.

Three of the young men approached Janelle, and just by watching her hands, the sisters knew that Janelle was having an animated discussion with the men. She was not what most people would consider beautiful, but she was so cute, and tiny. Her flip-flops were too large for her feet, but she liked to wear them that way.

She smiled at them all the while she was talking and when her face moved upward, they followed her gaze, seeing a drone flying overhead. It was small, probably being flown by someone nearby. Janelle scanned the beach homes and finally found the operator. She pointed toward the house and the men looked as well, getting waves from a forty-something man, wearing a Los Angeles Dodgers baseball cap, holding the controller in his hands.

While the guys were focused on the drone and the operator, Janelle walked away quietly. She was a good fifty feet away, when one of the young men began chasing her until he caught her and turned her around to face him.

2

Mansur Ahmad, a surgeon from Minnesota, on a two-week vacation, was enjoying the early morning calm as he flew his drone over the dunes, the beach, and high in the sky, getting a great view of the island. He watched small boats on the Sound, and people fishing from them. Larger boats were cruising in the calm water, and on one he was able to get a close-up of a gorgeous, young brunette sun bathing on the deck au natural. She was lying on her stomach and he fervently hoped she would turn over very soon. Within a minute or two, he got his wish and he stared at her full breasts and a lovely triangle of brown hair, just above long, long legs. She was a pretty girl too; he watched her for a moment and then returned the drone to the beach. There weren't many people on the sand at this early hour, but it wouldn't be long until the beach would be filled; that is, if the approaching storm missed them. His iPhone was capturing every image clearly. He was planning to email the video to his friend, Sameer Rahim, who was serving with the U.S. Army in Texas. Sameer was divorced, and a bit of a playboy, so he would probably enjoy the sun bather very much.

When he saw the woman in the green bikini, he flew a little closer to her. He was dangerously close to breaking the law, which could result in an $1100 fine, but he didn't care. She was stunning. Her skin was nicely tanned to a golden brown and her movements as she danced, pranced and cartwheeled, mesmerized him. He got the oddest feeling when she stared at him through her sunglasses-chills racing up and down his body; he couldn't take his eyes off of her. For some reason, she reminded him of his late wife, Sari.

Mansur lost his wife of fifteen years in February. She was walking down the road in front of their house, with their dog, Fazir, on a choker leash, by her side.

He was out in the yard, cutting the grass, when several shots rang out. He turned toward her and saw her slump to the side of the road clutching her chest. As the black SUV passed by her body, he saw the gunman point his weapon at him. Quickly, Mansur dove to the grass, curling up in a fetal position. Three rounds cut through the air over his head and then the car sped off.

He raced to her side, but she was already dead and he cried harder than he ever had. Fortunately Fazir survived, having only been slightly wounded.

The police investigated, but the shooter and driver were not found.

He flew the drone only inches from her face, really breaking all the rules, but he was hoping to see her eyes through the dark glasses.

3

"Uh-oh, girls, watch this," Lucinda said through her laugher."

Several moments later, the other two guys caught up to Janelle and their friend. One man grabbed Janelle's arm and Lucinda read her lips. "**Don't Touch Me, You Bastard!**" She screamed, loudly enough to turn a few heads, and then she uttered some more obscenities, causing the men to back off just a little. She stopped yelling, smiled, and then took off her sunglasses. The men ran away when they saw she had no eyes. Janelle laughed as she watched them run and stumble back to their tent, the dog, and the beer. She also saw the drone hovering above her, but never gave that a second thought.

Suddenly she felt her sisters and hurried toward them with smiles and waves.

She threw her arms around them. "I've been so looking forward to seeing you two. Because I am often alone, I've been trying to remember when we were to get together to reawaken and now I am so happy that time has come."

"We're happy to see you too, Janelle. You certainly put those young men in their places when they saw you without your glasses; no eyes, no eye sockets, just a face. They probably crapped themselves as they ran away." She looked at Amanda, seeing her chuckle.

"It wasn't the first time and I know it won't be the last, unless this ceremony provides me with real eyes, although I can see very well." As they started walking to the car, she said, "Last month, I saved two guys from falling off the roof of a building they were constructing. It was a gorgeous day, perhaps a bit warm, and no wind. I was walking down Lumina Avenue watching them work. The one young man handed a hammer to the other, and both lost their balance and fell toward the ground. I cast a time-freeze spell and hurried up to the roof to haul them back on top. I raced back down to the road and removed the spell; neither of them could believe that they hadn't fallen, when they were certain they did. Both of them saw me and I waved. They waved back, shrugged their shoulders and got back to work."

"That is quite interesting, Janelle. I didn't think you would have your other special powers back until we gathered by the Four Sisters tree tomorrow."

Lucinda looked toward the drone and then toward the porch the man was standing on. We need to get to him before he is able to send video of Janelle to the news media." The witches walked toward the beach home where Mansur stood.

Before leaving the beach, Lucinda mumbled some strange words and waved her hand, palm down, over everyone she could see, mass-hypnotizing them to forget everything they saw.

As they strolled up the sandy path over the dune, they came across a disgusting looking man in shorts and a t-shirt, his arms and legs covered with tattoos. His hair was long and unkempt and his eyes were glazed over, probably from the booze or the drugs he had recently taken. His black shirt bore the word HEATHEN.

Lucinda stopped in her tracks, as did her sisters and she said, "Are you really a heathen, young man?"

He snarled, "Who the hell wants to know, lady? You the question queen or something?" Saliva dribbled from his mouth.

"My friend, my sisters and I are good witches and we really despise your type of people; people who do not believe in the true God."

He laughed in her face. "Really! You claim to be a witch and yet you believe in God. That's a good one."

"Well, because we are white witches, and respect all religions, I am going to let you off with just a small spell." Lucinda mumbled a few words and moved her hands in front of the man.

A few moments later, he seemed to be confused as to where he was, and perhaps even who he was. Lucinda pointed to his shirt and the man looked down, seeing the word HEATHEN. He tore his shirt off, and fell to his knees, praying to the God he had turned his back on when he was fifteen. After praying he stood up and said, "I must go now. I think I have to return home to Alabama and see the pastor of the church where I once attended."

They all shook his hand and watched him walk back to the hotel he was staying in. He was actually humming an old hymn, one that they were all familiar with.

The witches walked into the doctor's condo, and he cowered in fear. Lucinda once again cast a spell and Mansur immediately forgot what he had just seen and videoed. Lucinda whispered in his ear and the surgeon nodded. The sisters left him and a moment later, he snapped out of it, not remembering anything, but knowing what to say if he was asked any questions.

Lucinda said to her sister, "I think we should immediately leave for Southport, have our ceremony soon, and then leave this area for a long time."

The girls nodded and they headed toward the car for the one hour drive to Southport.

The Evil Witches

Wilmington, North Carolina
July 10th, 2016

1

The triplets were having some fun, scaring people on the battleship North Carolina, loosening up their powers, hoping to catch their four sisters by surprise at the tree tomorrow morning.

Giselle McFadden, the oldest of the three by six minutes, was hiding in the bottom section of the old battleship, where the shells and powder canisters were located. Whenever a visitor or a group would be walking around, she would rattle some of the chains, levitate one of the large shells, or just let out blood-curdling screams, until she was alone again.

Being here, on this majestic battleship, gave her time to think about what happened back in 1944, and was the subject of a book in late 2014, titled *Fathoms.*

2

During World War II, a sailor disappeared from the ship during the Battle of the Marianas, when an American task force shot down about 500 Japanese planes and sank several of their ships, as well. After the battle, his buddies noticed that he was missing and a search was conducted throughout the boat. He was never found and presumed dead, having fallen overboard during the fight.

In 2014 his widow, his grandson, and granddaughter-in-law, along with some of his long- dead shipmates and some local people, solved the mystery of his disappearance.

Upon the discovery of his body, preserved in a cocoon of some kind of transparent, hardened jelly-like-substance, the government set out to recreate the material, but there was at least one component missing from the formula, and success eluded them

3

The following year, many miracles occurred to assign eight humans the task of sending all earthbound spirits to their final reward, be it Heaven or Hell. Four more humans joined the fight, and three of the twelve died, but everyone's lives were changed forever.

4

This area of the country had its fair share of paranormal experiences and in less than twenty-four hours, seven witches were scheduled to have their powers reawakened, but the triplets were going to make certain that only they would have the power, while their four sisters rotted in Hell.

Many years ago, Giselle told Lucinda that they would not be present at the Reawakening because the triplets didn't need to attend the ceremony, stating that their powers would never weaken under Satan. She laughed out loud, startling a 12-year old boy who was watching her from a few feet away. The boy was not frightened by her, even when she attempted to levitate him, and he would not rise: she didn't know what to make of this impossible scenario.

5

Twelve-year old Christian Balliet was given permission to explore the ship by himself, while his parents waited in the air-conditioned visitor center. Mike and Jamie Balliet were both claustrophobic and they trusted Christian implicitly. They gave him a two-hour time limit, and Jamie gave him her iPhone to take pictures or to contact Mike if necessary.

When Christian saw the beautiful, young woman, laughing like a hyena, he was startled, because she was well hidden and he didn't see her quickly enough to stifle his emotions. There was something about her that was not normal, but he wasn't the least bit scared. She attempted to levitate him, because he could feel her powerful pull, and he had to use his powers to counteract what she was trying to do.

6

Christian realized he was special when he was ten. He was strolling along the canal near his house, his dog Peko by his side, just enjoying the beautiful spring day. He grabbed a stick and threw it into the water, giving his two-year old Lab a chance to both swim and play. Peko grabbed the stick in his mouth and was paddling back when he disappeared beneath the surface. Christian had his mind on something else and when he saw Peko was gone, he got scared and dove into the cold, clear water, swimming beneath the surface, looking for his best friend.

Peko was trapped in a loop of cable wire and could not free himself. Christian hurried toward the frightened animal as he fought for his life and didn't know what to do. He knew he wasn't strong enough to break the steel cable and he saw the fear in Peko's eyes as the dog's air supply was nearing the end.

After praying for God's help, he felt a wave of energy wash over him. He looked into Peko's eyes, calming the dog, allowing for a little more time, although seconds only, perhaps. Christian placed his hands on the cable, and the loop holding Peko loosened enough for the dog to swim to the surface, breaking through the water into the sweet, cool air.

Peko gulped in oxygen and then swam to shore, waiting for his master to come out from the water. His dog mind tried to sort out what happened, but all he could figure was that he was trapped and Christian saved him. He also knew that there was no greater love than that of a person and his pet. Peko would live for thirteen more years and then die in Christian's arms.

7

Giselle conjured up a spell, hoping to turn the boy into a quivering, sobbing little kid, but that didn't work either.

"What are you, Boy? Are you a warlock? Have you been sent by my good sisters to keep us from stopping their reawakening?" She cackled and then attempted a disappearing spell on the boy, and again her efforts were thwarted.

Christian only smiled at her and then turned around, heading back up the narrow spiral stairs, looking back at her once, sending a charge of energy that singed some of Giselle's hair.

The witch stared back at him, totally amazed.

8

Marta Cullen, the second triplet to be born, was roaming through the enlisted sleeping quarters, swinging hammocks when visitors were going by. She had cast an invisibility spell on herself, so not only could she move the hammocks, she could also touch some of the people, causing them to recoil and scream out in fright. The visitors in her area headed back to the main deck and quickly left the boat, yelling to others, "Don't go down there! Ghosts are in the sleeping area and they scared all of us." They raced down the gangplank and drove away as fast as humanly possible.

Marta became visible again, watching a little boy saunter through the area, walking past her as though she didn't exist. Marta threw out her hands, sending a powerful wave of pure energy to knock the little squirt off his feet, but the boy turned around, held up his hands, palms toward her and pushed the energy back, knocking her off her feet.

"Don't try that again, Witch!" he yelled and then climbed the next set of stairs.

9

Bella Jansing stood on the bridge, creating havoc among the visitors below her on the deck. She conjured up a cloudburst, complete with thunder and lightning, causing thirty or forty people to scatter. As quickly as she started it, she stopped it. She saw dazed, confused faces on many of the visitors, and when they resumed their business again, she unleashed gators and snakes, which hissed and growled, striking out at the people, never touching them. She had no desire to kill anyone; she just wanted to have a lot of fun at the humans' expense. She cackled with joy as the people cried out in anguish, some of them wetting their pants and shorts.

Just as one young man was ready to tackle an alligator that was taunting a little boy of perhaps four, Christian appeared beside the witch and with a sweeping motion of his hands, he froze every person and creature on the deck.

When Bella saw him do this, she tried with all her might to break the spell the boy had just worked, but her power was not great enough to weaken the hold the child had on the people, gators, and snakes.

Trying a different tactic, she mumbled some words and shot bolts of energy from her hands toward him. He easily deflected them and then with a couple of swift motions of his hands, he made the creatures disappear, and wiped the minds of the people, so they had no memory of what had just occurred.

She faced him and said, "Who are you that you can possess stronger, more powerful powers than a four-hundred year old witch?"

"I am just a boy, who was sent by his Father to stop three evil witches from hurting innocent people. I am not here to do you any harm. Someone more powerful than I will see to your destruction."

The boy turned and walked away without another word, leaving Bella to contemplate his final words.

The Werewolves

Wilmington, N.C.
April, 2016

1

Several days after blowing up the restaurant where Hyram Lasky and his friends were celebrating, Adam, Eve, and Jamal moved into a beautiful, restored, Victorian home in Wilmington. The house sat on a hill overlooking the Cape Fear River and points south of the city.

They had taken new names; Eve was now Vicky Marsett. Adam changed his name to Jeffery Grandar, and Jamal would be known as Malcolm Clair. Adam and Eve's names were provided by Lynette Trexler, who was in charge of the facility where fifteen werewolf clones were being studied. The experiments went awry and the trio was forced to leave before they were captured or killed.

She and Adam had access to all of Lynette's finances and, after her demise they hacked into her bank accounts and wiped them out. Of course, where she was now, money would do her no good, Eve thought.

She felt such great joy when she, Adam, and Jamal planted three homemade IEDs under the tables and chairs where Lasky and his friends would be seated for what was to be a spectacular celebration of the detective's retirement. The trio hated him immensely because of his involvement with slaying the clones and closing the facility.

After Lasky arrived and sat at a chair facing the large window, the three pissed off bombers stood in front of the window, across the street, waiting for him to look out and see them. When he did, Eve smiled and waved goodbye.

They pressed the detonators and watched as the restaurant exploded from within. They saw glass, wood, and bodies flying about inside the building and a fire had started, as well. Satisfied that they had completed a successful mission and killed everyone inside, they dropped the detonators on the street and headed to Wilmington.

2

Vicky stared at the video for the umpteenth time, still not believing that Hyram Lasky survived the explosion, and the more she watched, the more furious she became. Someday she would go back to Bethlehem and finish him off, but right now she was having a difficult time with her pregnancy and she would have to delay her vendetta.

When she found out she was pregnant, two months ago, she located an obstetrician to take care of her. She read all she could find about human pregnancies and learned that the normal gestation period was usually nine months. Not realizing it would take that long she had to delay her revenge for an even longer period of time.

At two months, she figured her weight gain should be about two to three pounds, yet she had gained seventeen pounds and her stomach was much larger than normal for that period of time. She knew she would have to make an appointment to see the doctor even though Malcolm was studying all about childbirth. She was fairly certain that hers would not be a normal pregnancy and she wanted Malcolm to be prepared to help her with whatever she might need.

Vicky knew Malcolm had developed a brilliant mind after being scratched by one of the werewolves, and his appetite to learn had become insatiable. He knew how to do so many things, most of them illegal or unethical, but he felt he was one of the pack. He would do whatever it took to protect Vicky and the soon to be born child or children.

3

Jeff and Vicky patiently sat in the waiting room of Dr. Willis Little, Vicky's obstetrician, as the clock on the wall moved ever so slowly. He was behind, as usual, and the appointment time has passed by thirty-two minutes ago. The door finally opened, and Dr. Little summoned the couple into his office, he was shocked seeing Vicky's size. She looked like she was ready to go into labor soon.

He shook hands with Jeff as Vicky went behind a curtain to take off her clothing and put on a hospital gown. After she was dressed, she pulled the curtain open, stepped out from behind and hopped up on the examination table, her huge stomach impeding her movement quite a bit.

Dr. Little checked Vicky's vitals and then placed his stethoscope against her stomach at several places, hearing more heartbeats than what he thought was humanly possible. He thought the record for multiple births was about 9 but he wasn't certain. This pregnancy could go down in history and he could write a paper and perhaps become famous, finally erasing the stigma of having a spontaneous urination condition when he was younger, wetting his pants in public many, many times. His condition gave him the nickname, Leaky, and it followed him for his whole life since then.

His nurse, Serena Marshall, brought the ultrasound machine to the examination table and began scoping Vicky's stomach.

"Vicky, I'm going to rub this gel on you and then I'll take a transducer over your belly. The first trimester is when a doctor wants to check on the development of the fetus, or in this case, several fetuses to make sure everything is going okay. It won't hurt a bit," Serena said as she began the procedure.

Little watched the computer screen to see the ultrasound pictures of the babies. The sound the machine was making was unlike anything he or Serena had ever heard. He looked at her as she studied the computer screen. What they saw was impossible. The fetuses were not human; they looked like tiny dogs and there were eleven of them.

Serena's hands began to shake and she dropped the transducer after she felt them move around in Vicky's uterus.

Vicky held on to the sides of the table and parted her legs; her children were ready to be born and there was no stopping it from happening.

Dr. Little quickly rose from his chair, knocking it over as the tiny dogs, or possibly wolves, came into the world as Serena screamed. After each one was born, they began to grow until they were almost a foot long. At that point, their teeth were long enough and sharp enough to bite and they attacked the doctor and the nurse, swarming over them, tearing bits of flesh from their hands, legs, and faces. The screaming was ungodly loud. Vicky and Jeff feared passersby might hear the noises and come rushing in.

Jeff worked quickly and managed to muffle the doctor's and Serena's screams with towels, gloves and tape, stuffing their mouths and taping them shut as the tiny wolves continued tearing them apart. As he watched them writhe in agony, he called Malcolm to come with the van, explaining what had happened.

Darkness would fall in about an hour, so Jeff issued commands to the pups, settling them down. The physician and the nurse were dead, and the wolves became disinterested in their corpses, plus they were continuing to grow.

Now free of her burden, Vicky was able to move around without obstruction. She was bleeding heavily but gave it no thought. She had to protect the pups and get them back to the house without being seen. "Jeff, when Malcolm comes, we have to get the wolves out and burn this place to the ground. Open all the file cabinets so the records will catch fire and take the laptops with us when we go. We can't leave any evidence of us causing their deaths and where we live."

After Malcom backed into the driveway, he stepped from the van and opened the back doors. He quickly went inside and when the pups, now about three feet in length, saw him, they all stopped whatever they were doing and laid down resting their heads on their paws. He used only hand signals, but the wolf pups knew what to do and followed him out to the van and jumped inside. Since being scratched by a werewolf in January, so much had changed. Apparently he was now able to control other werewolves.

He closed the doors and went back into the doctor's office to help Jeff and Vicky prepare the place for a fiery death.

They grabbed the three laptops, opened every gas valve they could find and when the small office was filled with gas, they left the examining room. Malcolm lit a match and tossed in inside, quickly closing the door as the explosion damn near took it off. He raced to the van and drove off, watching the house go up in his rearview mirror. Inexplicably, nobody apparently saw them leave.

The Hunters

Causeway Café
Wilmington, North Carolina
July 11th, 2016

1

Sixty-two year old Aaron Pammer, a retiree from Mack Trucks and a resident of Hellertown, Pa., was the first to arrive. He looked inside the restaurant and saw a large table, set for twelve. He assumed this was where he would meet the others he had not seen in two years.

2

He remembered how he was designated to be one of the eight people selected by God, in the guise of George Burns, and the angel, Hannah, a ten-year old precocious child in life. Aaron was sleeping when he heard a clatter downstairs. He got up, took his .45 caliber pistol from the nightstand and stealthily went to investigate. He was glad his wife, Cindy, was out of town: in case something bad would happen, it wouldn't happen to her. New carpeting in the hallway and on the stairs muffled his footsteps as the noise in the kitchen became even louder. He wondered why in the hell an intruder, or intruders, would telegraph their presence by making so much noise in the kitchen.

When he reached the bottom of the staircase, the noise abated somewhat. He shook a little as he raised the powerful handgun, pointing it toward the kitchen. He padded across the living room, keeping a low profile; then he peeked around the corner into the kitchen. What he saw frightened him more than any intruder ever could.

Sunlight filtered into the small, neat kitchen, offering him a view of an impossible manifestation. He lowered his weapon, stood up, and gaped at the sight.

Every cabinet door and all drawers were open. The tea kettle and coffee maker were cooking away, although no heat was coming from the gas range and the coffee maker was not plugged in. The contents of the refrigerator were placed around the interior perimeter of the room. Utensils were mysteriously affixed to the cabinet doors.

Aaron quickly raced back upstairs to get his iPhone. He needed visual proof of all this, so nobody would think he had lost his mind. He hurried back down and once again went into the kitchen. When he got there, something new had happened. In the few minutes he was gone, all of the washcloths, tea towels, and linen napkins were incredulously fused to one another, creating a quilt of sorts and it was hung on the only bare wall in the room. He took his phone and created a video of floor, ceiling and walls. On the wall by the door, every knick-knack was turned upside down and backwards, some resting impossibly on the smallest part of each object. This was absolutely unbelievable, and his hands trembled even more than usual. For years he had been plagued by a neurological disorder known as essential tremors; but now his uncontrollable shaking would not stop.

The stacked articles resembled a horseshoe of sorts. The base item on each side were spatulas standing straight up with the flexible flipper pointing upward. On top of each spatula were Aaron's two small cast iron pans, well-seasoned after nearly one-hundred years of use, handed down to each generation. The handles pointed down, resting on the spatulas; spoons, knives, and forks were balanced on the edges of the pans, tines, scoopers and cutting edges pointed upwards. Balancing on them were many, many dinner plates, soup and salad bowls, and three gravy boats. The top of the horseshoe was a hodgepodge of baking pans, canisters, salt and pepper shakers, and jars of spices. He stared in wonderment at this assemblage of kitchen items pondering its meaning, when he heard something drop to the floor behind him. The noise startled him so that he grunted in surprise.

When he turned around, a phone number and a name appeared on the front of the refrigerator, put together with colorful number and letter magnets that had been stored in a drawer from when his daughter was a little girl.

He took a picture of the information; 910-555-7334 and CALL RICK CONLEN were stuck to the fridge. No sooner than he took the picture, the magnets crashed to the floor. He looked down, and when he looked up again, a new message appeared; YOU ARE NEEDED FOR THE GATHERING.

Aaron once again took a picture and then checked his phone to see if the video and photos were saved. They were. He punched in the numbers.

3

His life had changed dramatically since that day. After returning from The Gathering, where all the earthbound spirits were sent to their final reward-heaven or hell-he returned to Hellertown, energized. He told Cindy, his daughter, and the grandkids what had just happened, showing them the pictures he took in the kitchen that day and promised God to be more faithful and to volunteer for every opportunity he could do in his community and church.

63

Now he was back in North Carolina for another mission after receiving a call from George.

4

Kyle Quinlan was staying at a nice condo near the upper end of Wrightsville Beach. He had been confined to a wheelchair ever since a piece of shrapnel severed his spinal cord in Afghanistan many years ago, but that all changed in 2014 when he was so down-and-out that he couldn't find his way home one night from a bar in San Antonio, Texas. He was only three blocks away from his apartment, but he didn't remember which way to go.

Kyle heard what sounded like cannon fire and he saw flashes in the near distance. He turned his wheelchair around and rolled toward the noise. He looked to his left and right, seeing hundreds of soldiers, dressed in uniforms from long ago. They wore white pants, blue and red jackets, and high hats. When one of the soldiers reached down to pick something from the ground, Kyle saw a red circle on top of his hat. The soldiers were carrying long rifles, most with bayonets fixed.

They marched past him as though he wasn't even there and when he turned his head to the right, he saw more of them passing right through buildings and vehicles on the street as though the objects didn't exist.

He watched in fascination as they started running, some carrying makeshift ladders. Now Kyle knew he had finally cracked. He was watching Santa Ana's army attacking the Alamo, which he realized was only a couple of blocks straight ahead.

He grabbed both tires of the wheelchair, wanting to see a battle that was fought almost two hundred years ago, but his chair would not move. He was thrown off balance and he fell on the street, scraping his face and arms. When he looked up in frustration, wondering how he was going to get back in his chair, he saw the face he had seen all those years ago in Afghanistan. Jesus saved his life then and He offered a hand to Kyle. Kyle reached out and when he touched his Savior, he felt the nerves in his spine and his legs tingle with something like an electric current. Jesus pulled him to his feet and Kyle was healed, once again able to walk.

Jesus smiled at him and then disappeared.

The cannon fire and rifle fire became very intense. Kyle turned and began to run the last couple of blocks to the Alamo. He saw American volunteers firing from inside the structure, while Mexican soldiers climbed their ladders to get inside.

He watched this for several minutes and then the soldiers he could see, both inside and outside the walls began disappearing until there was nothing left but the silence of an empty street, a couple of hours before sunrise.

Kyle walked to the front door of the Alamo and stared at the graffiti written in what appeared to be blood on the large wooden entrance door. He read the message and immediately called the telephone number written in ten inch high numbers.

He went home and apologized to his wife, Julie, for all the times he let her down, and yet she stuck by him, praying every day that he would get help.

Kyle would never drink again.

As he stepped onto the parking lot in front of the Causeway Café, he saw two people he recognized immediately, exiting a 2017 BMW SUV.

5

Samuel and Samantha Staunton, 21-year old fraternal twins, from Bar Harbor, Maine saw Kyle and smiled. They remembered him so well and were looking forward to talking with him, and the others, too. Known as Sam and Sammy to their family and friends, the brother and sister had been stuck to each other like glue since they were kids. After losing their parents in a freak accident when they were ten, they grew even closer. Three weeks ago they celebrated their milestone birthday with a huge party, sipping their first legal drinks together in front of three-hundred and seventeen homeless and out-of-work residents in their home town. They provided food and drinks for all and before everyone left, they were each given a one-thousand dollar prepaid Visa card. Their lives changed two years ago, and they wanted to give back as much as they could to the less fortunate.

They often thought back to that fateful day in 2007

6

Before the accident, they were children of faith, attending Sunday school and worshipping at the local Presbyterian Church. Sam's childhood dream was to become a pastor and Sammy was leaning toward a career in medicine.

The family was on a day trip when a panel truck pulled out in front of them. Steven, the twins' dad, did everything he could do to avoid a collision, but he caught the left side of the other car, spun around, and crashed through a guardrail, hovering over the edge of a cliff, the car being held from falling by a small stump.

Other travelers stopped and tried to help, one guy telling them that the stump didn't look like it could hold the Honda Pilot too much longer. He opened the lift gate and the twins crawled to safety as the car moved forward a little more. Steve's wife, Stella, crawled over the console toward the back and stretched toward the young man, but she was just out of his reach. The vehicle shifted some more and the stump broke free. Sam and Sammy watched their parents plunge to the bottom of the cliff, the car exploding on impact.

From that day forward until they went on a camping trip, the twins never attended church services again, losing their faith completely.

7

On the first morning of their camping trip, Sammy unzipped the door to their tent and crawled out to the fire pit. Sam was already placing some kindling, which he took from a waterproof bag, on the top of the ash pile after moving some partially burned logs that had been wetted down to keep them from burning while the twins were asleep. He took a match to the raw wood as Samantha looked toward the southeast and saw a faint ribbon of red; the sun was still below the surface of the earth. She smiled because she and her brother would have a beautiful sunrise to witness here in northern Maine.

Once the kindling began to burn, he added some dry twigs and then a couple of split logs to the fire, bringing it up to roaring in no time. Though the air was relatively warm, a morning fire was necessary to brew their coffee. Samantha hooked the four cup coffee pot to the metal rod and placed the rod in the two Y shaped branches stuck into the ground on either side of the fire pit.

As it began to perk, with the scent of hazelnut coffee permeating the area, Sam took out his camera and attached a telescopic lens. A thin line of red from the still unseen sun bathed the mountain range with color, offering little light, but painting the sky with broader streaks of red. The terrain to his immediate front was still dark, but the approaching sunrise brought out the shapes of small shrubs, trees, and a small patch of wildflowers that were just beginning to show their colors. Sam snapped a shot, pleased with it.

When Sam smelled the fully brewed coffee he yelled out, "Sammy, please bring me a cup as soon as you can. It smells so good."

"You got it, Brother." She looked up to see the sun beginning to crest the craggy tops of the mountains, colored a deep blue. The sky above the sun was still deep blues and blacks, with the undersides of the clouds picking up the redness.

Sam took a few more shots and then he saw two people approaching.

"Sammy, two people are coming this way. I didn't know there was anyone else around,"

She knelt beside him. "Me neither. I wonder who they are and where they're camping. I didn't see any fires last night, did you?"

"No, Sis, I didn't. They're waving. Perhaps we know them. Guess we'll find out very soon."

The sun rose quickly and light danced in their eyes. It was so bright they had to shield their eyes with their hands. Over the course of the next few minutes, the sun became a burning white light. Sam thought how impossible that was, yet it was happening.

Temporarily blinded, neither of them could see the two people, probably less than twenty yards away.

Sam cupped his hands around his eyes and squinted, but all he could see were two shadowy figures, unrecognizable, even at this short distance. "Who's there?" He asked.

A moment or two later, the sun was blocked by the two people standing in front of them.

The twins were stunned. They couldn't believe their eyes.

Sammy gasped. "Mom? Dad? How?"

Stella said, "Hello, children. We have always been with you, but we weren't allowed to interact in your lives. You have both grown up to be fine young people, but you need to start living your lives again. Both of you need to find more friends and begin dating."

She reached out toward her daughter, but she was unable to touch her.

Her father pulled his wife's hand back. "We have been earthbound all these years. So close that we felt that we could touch you, and as you think back, you will remember those moments."

Sam said, "How is this all possible? I hope you're not going to say that this is all God's plan or some nonsense like that. We gave up on Him the day you two died and whatever this is, it can't be God that is doing this to us. We both must be hallucinating."

His father said, "No Son. You're not hallucinating. We were sent here today to tell you what God wants you to do." He pointed toward the sky behind them.

The twins turned and were given the privilege of seeing something that no human had ever been allowed to see. Heaven opened up and they saw angels and the face of God. They dropped to their knees and began to pray like they had never prayed before.

Lost in paying homage to God again after such a long time, they had no idea how long they had prayed, but after finishing, relishing their regained faith, they turned around and were disappointed to see their parents were gone.

After they went back to the campsite to pack up and go home, Sam saw a message painted on a rock. CALL RICK CONLEN. 910-555-7334

Sam took his phone from his pocket and punched in the numbers.

Now, two years later, they were back in North Carolina. The twins and Kyle walked up on the porch and shook hands with Aaron.

8

Bernadette Owen was stuck in traffic just a stone's throw from the restaurant. The drawbridge was up as a couple of tall sailboats were passing underneath on the Intracostal waterway. She turned the rearview mirror so she could see herself; something she had been doing for two years, ever since her leprosy-type condition disappeared from her body. She smiled at what the grace of God could do for people. She thought about her mom, who passed away just last year

9

Her mother was a prostitute, and her father was one of her Johns. Loretta Owen found out she was pregnant but she continued using drugs and alcohol in excessive amounts until about five months into her pregnancy. She prayed to God as hard, and as often, as she could, asking for a healthy baby. She quit her profession and got out of the life she was leading, beating her addictions to drugs, booze, and cigarettes. She moved to the suburbs of San Diego.

Loretta was fortunate, finding an apartment in a decent neighborhood that was easily affordable. Two days after she moved in she found a job answering phones and typing letters. Her boss's secretary was swamped and the idea of having Loretta help out, even for a few months, would give her enough leverage to get the office back in shape again.

The following week, she left work at lunchtime to meet with her new obstetrician. Dr. Riegger was an old college friend of her former doctor. He had no problem taking on a new patient and wanted to see her as soon as she was settled. Unfortunately, he was ill the week she moved in.

Ten days later, after the exam, he said, "Loretta, everything looks good. The baby has a strong heartbeat and she is quite active in there. Your weight is a little higher than I would like, but not dangerously so. Just lay off the ice cream for a while and I think you'll be fine."

One day at work, a couple of months later, she started getting labor pains about a month early and she was taken to the hospital by ambulance. Dr. Riegger was already scrubbed by the time she arrived. After a quick exam, he determined that the baby was turned and was having difficulty. He was certain the umbilical cord was wrapped around the baby's neck and wanted to get the child out immediately by cesarean section. Loretta agreed and minutes later she was in the OR.

When Dr. Riegger delivered Bernadette, he turned pale and didn't know what to say. The nurse and the anesthesiologist had to look away. Much like a leper, the child's body was covered with discolored patches of skin. Her face was the worst, giving the impression that her skin had been burned off of eighty percent of her head. Even the baby's lips were not immune to whatever the hell it was that Bernadette had.

He handed Bernadette to Loretta and she didn't know what to expect by the look on his face. When she saw her baby, she smiled through her tears. Although Bernadette did not look normal by any means, Loretta was sure that her imperfection was part of God's plan and that someday, she would do something very important.

Loretta took Bernadette home and cared for her, watching her grow by leaps and bounds. When she took her outside, people shied away. The few friends she had limited their visits to a few minutes and after a couple of months, the visits ended.

One day while she was food shopping, she dropped some items from her hands and a man helped her pick them up. They talked a little while, pushing their carts side-by-side, and he helped her put her bags into her car.

"Would you have time for a cup of coffee or a bite to eat before you have to go home?"

Loretta didn't expect an invitation from him, because she hadn't had a man's company in a long time. Nobody would ever watch Bernadette, so when she went out, she tried not to stay longer than an hour. She knew God would protect her baby for the short periods of time she was out of the house. She decided to be honest with him and said, "I have a six-month old baby girl at home and she is alone. I don't like to spend too much time away from her."

"Why must you leave your child alone, Bernadette?"

"I have no one to care for her, and I don't bring her with me too often. You will know what I mean when you see her."

He nodded and smiled. "It's okay. I understand, but I really would like to spend some time with you."

"Well, if you don't mind coffee and toasted cheese sandwiches, we could go to my apartment and I'll make lunch for you."

"I'd like that, Loretta."

He followed her to her apartment and helped her carry her groceries inside. Fortunately he didn't buy anything that needed refrigeration so he was able to leave his stuff in his car.

She unlocked the door and after they stepped inside, they heard Bernadette cooing. "My daughter is different from other kids and if you are appalled by her, you may certainly leave and there will be no hard feelings."

When she brought Bernadette out, the smile never left Gene Ramsey's face. Bernadette saw him smile and reached out for him.

Loretta handed her baby to him and she hugged him hard. He played with her for the entire time Loretta was busy putting away her groceries and making lunch.

Eight months later they were married.

Gene was what wealthy people would call comfortable at the time he met Loretta and Bernadette. They took Bernadette to numerous doctors and clinics hoping to discover a way to restore her skin, but after years of fruitless search, they realized there was no hope for her. They home-schooled her and kept her out of the public eye as much as possible, but, now sixteen, Bernadette wanted to learn how to drive and go to regular school and meet kids her own age.

She finally got her way and not long after she got her license, they gave their permission for her to take the car and do whatever she wanted to do, but to call them if she had any problems with people making fun of her or being mean in any way.

Bernadette came home less than two hours later, tears streaming down her face. Everyone she saw laughed at her, or cringed when they saw her face, arms, and legs. A photographer took pictures of her as she raced back to the car, and she thought someone took a video of her too.

She realized that she had to go back to home-schooling, but when she graduated two years later, she was ready to try the outside world again.

Gene talked often about an uncle who had served aboard the aircraft carrier Midway and Bernadette searched the great ship on the Internet. The more she read, the more fascinated she became with its history. Not too long afterward, it was announced that the Midway would be berthed in San Diego and become a museum. She wrote to the president of the museum and told him how much she would like to be employed on the ship but she would like to work nights because of her skin condition. She enclosed a picture of herself, something she had never done before. Several weeks later, she was contacted and asked to come in for an interview.

10

Two years ago, she was walking around on the flight deck around 3 AM. The night was calm and stars filled the sky. It was a perfect time of the day for a person to reflect on life and just enjoy God's world.

The quiet was shattered by the sound of an approaching jet. She searched the sky but could not see anything, yet it sounded like it was almost on top of her. Without warning, an F-14 Tomcat landed on the deck with a squeal of tires. She approached it and when she touched it, her hand passed through the fuselage. She quickly pulled her hand out and nearly screamed when the cockpit opened and two transparent figures scurried down the ladder.

One exclaimed, "Miss, Rick Conlen needs you!" He pointed to a series of ten numbers painted on the side of the plane. In the distance she could hear the roar of what sounded like many, many planes. She looked up and out, toward the noise and in moments, a large number of aircraft, prop planes, choppers and jets passed over the Midway and then circled back, preparing to land. She knew just about every type of aircraft that had been assigned to the carrier over the years.

She grabbed her iPhone and punched in the number.

11

A loud horn rang out behind her; the traffic had begun to move across the bridge and she was still idling. She waved back to the person and put her car in gear, turning into the parking lot of the Causeway Café a couple of minutes later.

12

Six cars behind Bernadette, Rick Conlen and his wife Denise waited for the boats to pass beneath the drawbridge, as well.

13

Two years ago, Rick was out for a run and when he stood near the center of the drawbridge, he witnessed something remarkable and unbelievable at the same time. He called Denise, who was in their apartment at the Carolina Temple

Island Inn where they were staying for a long weekend and she quickly drove to the bridge, about a mile and a half away.

As he stood at the center of the bridge, talking to Denise, he could hardly believe his eyes. Three large, wooden sailing ships from a time long past were not quite sailing in the water toward the bridge, but rather were moving on a thin layer of air about a foot above the surface. He watched people aboard each vessel performing the functions that would probably be executed on an everyday basis, had these ships been filled with living crew members.

A man, dressed in a very expensive-looking suit, highly polished shoes, a pink dress shirt and a black, silk tie, rushed to the railing. "Oh, my God! The first ship is the USS Hunter. It sank in 1861 somewhere off the Outer Banks and took nearly one-hundred men with it to the bottom." He strolled back and stood beside Rick. My great-something-grandfather perished on that ship. I hope I can recognize him if I see him. His picture has been hanging in our house forever." Moments later, he did indeed see him.

The second vessel looked quite a lot like the pictures he had seen of the Nina, Pinta, and Santa Maria. Five sails were filled with wind, propelling it forward, yet there was no wind to speak of. The sails were adorned with Spanish markings, so chances were this ship could have been part of a fleet or an armada. Rick leaned toward the latter because he saw cannons protruding from the one side, and he was sure the same would be found on the other side. Again, this ship was filled with ghosts, waving their hands, hats, and pieces of cloth. The sound of laughter was carried toward the bridge on the non-existent wind. He realized it was the Santa Maria when he saw the spirt of Christopher Columbus smile at him. The Santa Maria was Columbus's personal ship.

The third ship was a whaler from the mid-nineteenth century. There were crewmen raising a long dead translucent whale from the water. It was the first time Rick had ever seen the spirit of a mammal and he wondered if more of God's creatures would show themselves in their ghostly forms. As he continued to watch the ghosts of sailors retrieve the ghost of the whale, Denise had finally worked her way to the center of the bridge and took his hand.

"Rick, this is really crazy, isn't it? Not only the spirits that are rising, but the number of people that are witnessing this event is amazing."

He nodded. "Crazy isn't the word, Denise." He pointed toward the trio of ships nearing the drawbridge. I'm rather curious to see what's going to happen when this first ship tries to pass beneath with the drawbridge down. They do look solid, don't they?"

Denise stared at the first ship, less than twenty feet from the bridge, its sails much higher than the closed drawbridge. It did appear solid and she thought she could even hear the sails ruffle, though there was no wind. She hadn't noticed that when she arrived, but the sails were surely filled with air, propelling the ships at a fairly rapid speed.

Moments later, the upper portions of sails passed through the bridge, exiting on the far side.

Rick and Denise reached out and tried to touch rippling sails, wooden masts, small flags, ropes, and their hands passed through everything. Several young kids, not fearful of anything it seemed, raced through the sails, masts, flags and ropes. One of them said, "That tickles, let's do it again." He and his friends crossed through the ghost ship to the other side of the bridge. Unbeknownst to anyone at this time, two days later the boys would all be dead.

After the three sailing ships passed under and through the bridge, followed by many more ships and smaller craft, the excitement left the crowd. Most everyone headed back to cars, trucks and bicycles. Those who walked or ran went back to doing that, but they would never forget what they had seen today, even though very few people would believe them. Their phones and cameras would not record any of the strange occurrences.

Rick and Denise were shocked that all the witnesses just left, and also that there was no mention of this in any media source However, these questions and many more would be answered very soon.

14

The morning was so nice that Hyram and Susan decided to walk to the Causeway Café for breakfast and then take a run afterward. They were enjoying their vacation so much and really liked the people that were staying at Steve and Mary's place. They saw an interesting bicycle-like vehicle passing by on the other side of the street. After Googling different bicycles, he found out it was a stand-up elliptical bicycle and it was really cool.

They approached the porch of the Causeway Café and saw a bunch of people looking toward them, almost like they were expecting them to come here this morning. Hyram felt the hairs on the back of his neck stand up, and he was afraid he was about to become involved in another paranormal event. He looked over at Susan and saw she had a queasy kind of look on her face, too. Before they climbed the stairs the porch, a very old man, smoking a cigar, and a child of about ten, greeted them.

"Hyram and Susan, I am so glad you took my message to heart and decided to join us today. We have a big job ahead of us and I don't think we could do it without you two."

After studying the man, dressed in a red button-down shirt, white golf knickers, red, white and blue long socks, red and white saddle shoes, and a blue Ben Hogan style cap, wearing thick glasses, Hyram said, "Do I know you? You look so familiar." He knew nothing of a message from this man.

"You do indeed know me, although you never met me in the flesh before. I am God, and I am in my disguise as a George Burns lookalike. I chose this disguise two years ago because I truly liked the way the late, great actor portrayed me in the movie, *Oh God.* He really made me laugh. You may call me George and this young lady is one of my top angels. Her name is Hannah."

Hy and Susan were stunned and, perhaps, in disbelief.

George noticed their discomfort and as he took a hand from each of them into his, they felt more comfortable than ever before in their lives. "When we are seated, all the people standing behind me are going to tell you both some incredible stories, but believe me, they are all true. So what do you say we head inside and get some food in our bellies? This place has the best shrimp and grits I have ever eaten, and all their other food is great, too."

Hy and Susan were astonished that God would have to eat, and they shrugged their shoulders, giggling like school kids.

15

Everyone introduced themselves and after their orders were placed and beverages brought to the table, small talk ensued until their meals arrived. They ate and drank with gusto as the conversation continued, and when the table was cleared, George stood up and said, "It's time for some serious talk now, so hold onto your hats, everyone, and watch what happens." George waved his hands, palms down, in a three-hundred and sixty-degree circle and everyone in the restaurant was frozen in position, some a bit awkward, garnering some laughter from the diners at the long table. "Please write down the exact time, to the second, on your phones, or set your stopwatch capability when I count to three." He counted and they responded.

"I didn't want anyone to listen in on our conversation, so they will be frozen until we finish." He explained why they were all gathered together, causing Hyram and Susan to gasp when he said that there were werewolves in Wilmington, along with witches, and more earthbound spirits. Our mission is to rid the earth of these creatures, and I have once again assigned you all the job. Hy and Susan are new to us, but they have dealt with werewolves and a vampire, in their time. They have skills and knowledge to help us in this great battle." While he spoke, the door opened with a creaking sound and a twelve-year old boy came and sat down at the table. "Friends, this is one of my sons, Christian Balliet, and he is going to pitch in, too. In fact, he already has had confrontations with three witches."

16

Acting as a waitress, Hannah returned to the table with several carafes of coffee, and individual creamers. She also brought a couple of pitchers of water and one of orange juice because the conversation was going on for a very long time.

Each ghost hunter shared his or her story, including what they had been doing the last two years. Hyram and Susan listened intently, occasionally asking a question. Because Hy and Susan lived in Bethlehem and Hellertown, they truly enjoyed listening to Aaron Pammer's story about the structure on his kitchen table and how other items were laid out on the floor. They looked over the pictures with great interest, trying to visualize him seeing this in his house.

Bernadette's and Kyle's stories really captured their attention. Two people who had maladies and injuries that were incurable, yet Bernie was a beautiful young lady and Kyle had use of both of his legs after having a spinal cord severed. To Hy's knowledge, you didn't come back from that one. No superglue in the world could repair an injury that devastating. He was becoming a true believer that George was actually God and when he thought that, from the corner of his eye, he saw George turn his head and nod at him, smiling. That was a little weird.

He was sad, though, that Kyle once again had the use of his legs. Hy's were gone, along with an arm, and Susan lost an arm. Would God give them back their limbs after this mission was completed? He looked toward George who gave no indication he was listening to those thoughts.

17

Susan listened with great interest: plus she had her notebook out and was jotting down names, numbers, places, quotes, anything she could use in the story she hoped she would write about this mission. The assignment to send the spirits away was called The Gathering, but so far, no name was given to this task. She thought of a couple and wrote them down, in case she could use one of them.

18

George stood up to re-introduce Rick and Denise Conlen. Susan couldn't wait to hear their stories, especially after catching a couple of snippets during breakfast. She poured a cup of coffee, and when she reached for the creamers, she noticed a couple of plates of doughnuts and other pastries and wondered where they came from. She grabbed a small glazed doughnut and realized it was one from Brit's at Carolina Beach. She and Hy drove down there the night before last and each of them ate a half dozen. They were the best doughnuts they ever ate. She figured God was working in one of his mysterious ways.

19

Rick Conlen took his turn to share his story. Many of the ghost hunters had not heard what he had gone through a couple of years back, so he decided to start with how he had become blind.

I'd been blind since the age of fourteen. I tumbled down a hill while skiing and hit my head on a rock. What I didn't tell you, or anyone, as a matter of fact, was that just before I fell, I saw a pinpoint of bright, white light, the brightest light I've ever seen and I was mesmerized. The faster I skied down the hill, the closer and larger the light grew until it took on the shape of a door." He paused for several moments and then after a deep breath, he continued. "I looked through the light and saw my grandfather, who had passed on when I was nine. It appeared as though he was waving to me, until I realized he was working his hands in a pushing motion, waving me away instead of in. I had never felt so at peace, and I thought God was ready for me.

"My grandfather appeared to try to vigorously push me away from the light. I knew I wasn't ready to join him and the others I could see. One of the people, for lack of a better term, I saw, was dressed in Confederate gray. He had a dirty, bloody bandage wrapped around his head and his left eye. His uniform was in tatters and his left leg was gone, just above the knee. He must have been so afraid when he died because his eye was open so wide, as though he was screaming. It chilled me to the bone.

"With each passing second, the door loomed larger and I feared I would pass right though it and disappear from the face of the earth. I couldn't leave my family like that, so I bent my knees and leaned all the way to the left until I felt my weight lifting my skis off the ground and I began to tumble. I prayed that I would not die, and asked God to forgive my sins and allow me to continue His work here on earth, whatever He wanted me to do."

Rick took a sip of water and cleared his throat.

"I felt myself tumbling down the hill, seeing the partially snow-covered boulder five feet away. I steeled myself for impact, trying to turn my head away from the stone, hoping I would survive. When I hit it, I lost consciousness. Two days later, I awakened and I saw someone at the foot of my bed. He was dressed in clothing from the early twentieth century. He told me he was an earthbound spirit, who had not yet been able to find his way to the afterlife. I swiveled my head from side to side and only saw blackness, yet he came through so clearly. I didn't know what I was supposed to do, but after he told me how he died, he disappeared from my sight. I went back to the darkness that would be the rest of my life, I thought.

"I never told anyone about him, nor the many spirits that have found me during my lifetime. Once they told me how they died, or the major sin they committed, that kept them earthbound, they would disappear. During these encounters, I kept believing that my sight was coming back, because I was beginning to see shadows.

"I had been visiting my eye doctor, Elliot Mayotte, once I began to see shadows and every exam he gave revealed that that would be all I would ever see. Then one day, Denise and I were sitting by the waterfront and something remarkable happened.

20

"We were sitting on a bench, just enjoying the beautiful day when I said, 'We have company.' She was finally getting used to me telling her this. There even had been times that when the spirits wanted her to see them, they showed themselves. I think the first time that happened, it almost scared the crap out of her."

Everyone laughed, and Rick gave them a couple of minutes to reload the coffee or tea cups and fill their water and juice glasses, as well. He looked at the center of the table and now, along with the doughnuts and pastries, there were also more eggs, bacon, and grits. He shook his head and chuckled. When plates and cups were refilled, he continued.

"His name was Cecil Goodwin. He was a boilerman on the North Carolina during the war. In Sixty-one, not too long after the ship was moored across the river, he looked over and saw some of his buddies, who had perished onboard, wave to him. The sight scared him to death, and he's been haunting this area ever since.

"'So what does he want from you? Denise asked me. I really had no clue. As I waited for him to tell me what he wanted, he materialized, scaring a neatly bearded, bald man, sporting rings in each ear. He was carrying a fishing rod and a white bucket; both fell from his hands. The bucket bounced and came to rest at Denise's feet. It was empty.

"Regaining his composure, the man stammered, 'What's going on here?' He pointed to Cecil. 'He just appeared out of thin air.' I saw Cecil smile and he said, 'I'm a freaking ghost, Sonny. Now get your stuff and leave or I will haunt you forever.' The man picked up his bucket and rod and trotted away, pausing to look back once to see the spirit draw a finger across his throat"

Even though she lived it, Denise had to laugh hearing Rick tell the story, and then Rick laughed too.

"When I turned my attention back to Cecil and then looked at Denise, I gasped. I was beginning to see her more clearly than in the past several weeks. She saw the look on my face and said, 'You okay? You look like you saw a ghost.' Shaking her head at the stupidity of that, she laughed. 'I think I'm losing it.' She even saw Cecil smile.

"I said, 'Yeah, I'm fine. I think I may have turned my head too quickly and a little pain took me by surprise.' I wanted to talk longer as I studied her features, still a bit cloudy, but it sure seemed like my sight wanted to come back, and all I could hope is that when I regained full vision, if ever, I would get myself checked out.

"I turned to Cecil and asked why he was still earthbound. He smiled and said to Denise, 'You sure are pretty. My wife was a very attractive woman. I was thirty-nine when I died. She was thirty-seven then and my death ruined her. She turned to alcohol to ease her pain and died penniless and homeless at forty-two. Fortunately, she never became earthbound and I truly hope that when I can leave this state, I will see her again.' He paused, stood up and pointed to the ship. Three specters were waving to him. He looked back toward Rick and Denise. 'Those are my buddies. I think I might be earthbound because I'm still connected to them and I don't know how to break free from the pull of the spirits still on the ship. They have been aboard for a long time. How can we move on, Mr. Conlen?'

"I shrugged my shoulders. 'Cecil, I'm afraid I can't answer that right now, but perhaps someday you will all be able to move on. I've been studying this subject for as long as I've had this gift of ghost whispering. I've set up a website and a Facebook page to find others like me, but no luck so far. Just hang in there and we'll see you again.' We stood up and began to walk away. Denise said goodbye to Cecil and quickly caught up with me, slipping an arm through mine. When I looked at her, her face was becoming even clearer and I was amazed with the whiteness of her teeth. Her eye color was still hazy and there were gaps in her features, and I was getting anxious for that moment when I would see all of her. I'm getting a little emotional, gang, so I think I will let Denise finish the story."

21

"Hi everyone. I guess I should start at the beginning, too. The day I met Rick he was sitting at an outdoor table in front of The Pharmacy, a restaurant where I was a waitress. A young couple from Pennsylvania, Brandon and JoAnne Pederson, were having a couple of drinks at the bar, when I saw an old man and a young woman waving me over to their table. I went over and took their order and they also wanted to buy a round for the Pedersons.

"I grabbed two drinks and put them on the counter in front of the Pedersons and then turned toward the refrigerator. Brandon said, 'We didn't order another round.' A moment later, bottles and glasses broke. I turned around and was going to tell them about the couple buying them one, and when I looked, probably no more than thirty seconds later, they were gone. I raced outside and looked both ways, not seeing them, pissed off because they left without paying their bill. I saw a man sitting at one of the outdoor tables, working on his laptop. I said, 'Excuse me, Sir, but did you see a bearded older man and a young woman come out from the restaurant?' He turned his face toward me. 'No, I didn't see anyone but I'm sure they could not have passed by without me hearing them.' His dark sunglasses hid his eyes.

"I saw a dog lying by the man's feet and a folded cane was on the table beside his computer. 'Oops,' I blurted out before even realizing it. He smiled and said, 'I guess you've figured out that I am blind.' 'Yes, I did and I'm so sorry for jumping to conclusions.' He laughed, washing away the tension I was feeling and then he said, 'No problem. I'm Richard Conlen.' When he felt the dog rise and place his head on his leg, he ruffled his German Shepherd's hair. 'This is Riley.' I shook Rick's hand, and felt a jolt of electricity. The tingle actually felt good, and I squeezed his hand a little tighter."

She looked at Rick and saw he was getting a little red, and then she continued with her story.

"He told me I had a pretty good grip and said, 'So do you have a name, Superwoman?' I laughed and told him my name. Than he asked, 'So, strongwoman Denise, why do you need to find the couple you think just left?' I told him what had happened inside and thought they were trying to stiff me and The Pharmacy for their bill. I told Rick I was puzzled by how quickly they disappeared. Then I remembered I had to clean up the mess and take care of my customers, but I asked him if he wanted a drink. He told me he'd like any kind of beer."

She took a sip of coffee, wondering if she should share what she felt at that moment and decided she should. "I had a feeling I was going to be connected to something that would scare the hell out of me, or bring out the best of what I had to offer. One of the busboys cleaned up the mess and after the Pedersons left, I took a break and went outside with Rick's beer and one for myself. He told me about the accident that took his sight at fourteen, and that he went to law school and was one of the few blind lawyers in the country. He laughed and said, 'Guess that proves that justice is blind.'

"Later that afternoon, I went to Rick's office and was stunned and scared shitless when I heard Rick speaking, but nobody was there. A couple of minutes later, five ghosts revealed themselves to me and that is when I found out that Rick was not only a blind lawyer, but he could actually see ghosts. He was a ghost whisperer.

"To make a long story short, the Pederson's became an integral part of our lives for the next several days. Brandon's grandfather disappeared from the U.S.S. North

Carolina during the Battle of the Marianas Islands in 1944, and he became possessed by his grandfather's spirit. We were able to help the couple and eventually we discovered where Al Pederson's remains were and they were brought home to Wilkes Barre, Pennsylvania." She turned to Rick and asked if he would like to tell the rest of the story.

22

Rick excused himself to go to the bathroom, working his way around the still-frozen figures. One waitress was going to stumble over something on the floor when she was brought back, so he picked up the wallet and placed it on a table, where a man had his hand outstretched, looking toward the wallet on the floor.

It was quite eerie, even for a ghost whisperer to see human statues, and he wondered how much time had passed by already. He figured it must have been close to an hour and after he finished what he had to say, Hyram and Susan were going to tell their stories. He also wondered what God's Son was going to offer.

At the table, the ghost hunters, and Hy and Susan, were filling their plates again, as the table was filled with more breakfast fare. The coffee pots were seemingly unending, and even though they had only eaten a short time ago, most everyone was hungry again.

George, Hannah, and the boy were talking quietly to themselves, and the room was filled with the air of mystery-what would the new mission be.

23

When Rick returned to the table, everyone finished what they were chewing or drinking to give him their complete attention.

"I didn't tell Denise that the two people who bailed on the check wouldn't have been able to pay her, anyway, since they were long dead." He saw the expression on her face, and then she smiled.

"On the day I went to visit Dr. Mayotte, I was very nervous. I saw as well as anyone, I guess, and I didn't want to lose my sight again. He did some tests and then used a machine to see the optic nerve. Mine was severed and I should not have able to see a thing, but my eyesight was perfect. You see, an optic nerve cannot be re-connected, so I should have remained sightless for the rest of my life." He nodded at George, who simply closed and then opened his eyes. After recovering from his disbelief, Elliot heard a noise in the outer office and excused himself to see what the devil it was. He opened the door to the reception area and saw a young girl sprouting wings, a Confederate soldier, and an old man. Elliot smiled believing that I had regained my vision through Divine intervention and no exam in the world would ever change that result. He nodded at the specters and stepped back into the exam room.

"After my appointment with Elliot, I returned to the office. Denise was at her desk feverishly working on a ten-inch high stack of letters. She had removed them all from their envelopes and I watched her at work. She picked up a letter, quickly read it and then typed a response on a word document. She finally noticed me standing there and swiveled her chair. She said, 'So where have *you* been while I've been at my desk working my fingers to the bone while you're out lollygagging somewhere, not telling me where.

What's the deal, Conlen? Playing blind man's bluff in the traffic?' After she said this, a rousing laugh from the ghosts burst out at the table.

After they settled down, Rick continued. "She said, you know I worry about you when you go out and don't tell me where you're going.' I smiled at her and said, 'That's a beautiful yellow sundress you're wearing. The color looks so good next to your tan, and I must add, very long legs. I love the way you styled your hair, and your eyes are soooo green! I don't think I've ever seen a more beautiful woman than you. I think I'm going to have to marry you someday.' She sat there with her mouth wide open, not knowing what to say. A moment later she understood that I was able to see her. She jumped up from the chair, rushed toward me and kissed me hard. 'How?' she asked.

"I shrugged my shoulders. I don't understand how, but I think each time I saw a ghost, my sight returned a little bit more. I could see everything yesterday when we were out. Full vision returned after seeing Cecil, but I wanted to see Elliot this morning. He assured me that he saw nothing that would cause me to become blind again. Not too long after that, I began getting calls from the people at this table, and you have all heard their stories. Thanks for your attention."

24

George motioned to Hyram and he immediately stood up; he actually felt like he rose from his chair without using his legs. He figured George was making things a little bit easier.

"Hi folks, I'm Hyram Lasky, a retired police detective from Bethlehem, Pennsylvania, and this is my girlfriend, Susan Mitchell. She's a reporter for the Saucon Valley Press in Hellertown, a small town that borders my city. I'm certain most, if not all, of you are up to snuff on what we faced in

Pennsylvania over the past six and a half years, with a vampire, and then werewolves terrorizing the city, so I'm going to be brief.

"Steve and Mary Wright paid for us to have a nice vacation in Wrightsville Beach, at their Carolina Temple Island Inn. If you have never stayed there, I highly recommend it. It is one of the coolest places we have ever stayed. Not only is there a great porch where we had cocktails almost every late afternoon, they have a 'pet' squirrel named Fred, who can be pretty amusing." Hy debated whether he should tell them that Fred spoke with him a couple of times, but he figured he'd save that conversation for another time. Things were pretty strange to begin with.

"Back in 2010, a vampire terrorized Bethlehem and when all was said and done, it was killed. We learned that it was under a witches spell for a hundred and fifty years and if it could kill five beautiful young women between Black Friday and Christmas Eve, the curse would end and the vampire would become human again. On Christmas Day, our coroner found a couple of bodies in a field. They were torn to shreds and when we followed tracks that appeared to have been made by very large wolves, they turned into human footprints and led us to an underground tomb. Those were the only people killed, although I continued to watch and worry that on any full-moon, the wolves could strike again. It didn't happen again until the day after Christmas in 2015, when a female werewolf killed a young Lehigh University student. The terror was upon us again.

"A secret facility was discovered where fifteen werewolf clones were created. Certain radical military leaders, scientists and a woman by the name of Lynette Trexler were attempting to turn these creatures into soldiers. Things went awry and thirteen clones, plus the

92

original three lycanthropes escaped and were finally killed. Two of the clones became human, killed Miss Trexler, and escaped. Along with a young black man, named Jamal, they left the area and the search has been going on since that day, but they have not been sighted and we have no clue where they are. I don't know why George and Hannah included us in whatever mission they're planning, but I guess Susan and I will find out soon. Thanks."

25

George stood up to address the hunters. "I made certain that you would all be here at this specific time because this mission will be a great challenge to everyone. Once again earthbound spirits are wandering around in huge numbers, and they need to be sent away before they begin creating mischief. Too many people are getting frightened by these specters, so again I call on my ghost hunters.

"Hyram and Susan are here because recently Adam and Eve became the parents of eleven werewolves and I can't let them roam around the city unabated. Those two, along with Jamal, were the ones who created the explosion that took limbs from Hyram and Susan, killing and injuring twenty-three people. They have new names, now, but they will not be easy to find. They might even find you both, Hy and Susan, because tomorrow they will know that you are here.

"What do you mean by that, George? Obviously you know everything, but how will our presence here become known to them?"

"The reporter that was with you all at Steve and Mary's place wrote an article and his editor deemed it newsworthy enough to print, so your names and pictures will be on the front page of the morning paper."

"Why don't you just use your power to keep them from getting to us? I'm not afraid for Susan and myself, but there are innocent people staying at the Inn and they could get hurt by them very easily. I don't know what Jamal can do, but I fear that since he was scratched by a werewolf, he could become one at any time."

George nodded. "That is so true, but it is part of my plan to separate them from their children. I'm going to have the wolves board the North Carolina along with the ghosts. Right now, three evil witches are locked there, courtesy of my Son." Christian nodded and smiled."

Kyle raised his hand and George gave him a nod. "We know how to fight earthbound spirits, but how will we fight werewolves and witches? These are the things you want us to do, but what will we use for weapons?"

"When you all return to your rooms, everything each of you need will be there. You will know what to do with them at that time. I know every one of you are prepared to do battle again, and if no problems occur, you will probably all survive."

The hunters began whispering among themselves, and within a few minutes all agreed that they would complete this mission for God.

Susan stood up and asked, "We know that Hannah is one of your angels, but she is very young. Why did she have to die, George?"

George glanced toward Hannah and the angel stood up.

26

"I've been an angel since 1912. I died after the Titanic went down. My mother was with me, but my father stayed behind, to show the other men that he was not afraid to die, so others could live. He helped rally many women and children to the lifeboats, and as Mother and I were lowered into the water, I watched him help those women and children get into the boats. He saw a man try to hop aboard and he yanked the man by his coat and pulled him back to the deck. Several passengers and crew applauded him and the would-be coward stood up and ran toward the other side of the ship. I didn't know if he got off or if he died until I saw him bound to earth as a spirt after I died.

"We were several hundred yards from the ship and heard the screams of the dying as the great ship lifted out of the water and then broke in half. It was the most horrific sound I ever heard in my ten years of life. The screeching of metal breaking apart was incredibly loud and the ship lights were disappearing as the electrical circuits became water logged. Once the ship sank, there was an ungodly...oops, sorry, George, silence." Many of the people chuckled, breaking the tension that they felt hearing Hannah's story.

"We floated in our lifeboat for a long time, hearing screams from passengers in the water. Soon there were no sounds in the ocean anymore, only the suffering we all felt as we waited for rescue or death.

"Mother had been sleeping and when she woke up, she began thrashing about, becoming less lucid with her speech. I held onto her, trying to calm her down, but she fought me off and fell overboard. I cried out, 'Lord, let me save her and I will be indebted to you forever.' I stood up and dove into the freezing water, the cold almost taking what little breath I had away. I strained my eyes trying to locate her and suddenly a luminescent area appeared to my left and I saw her, struggling in her heavy clothes. I kicked hard and swam to her, lifting her from the depths, managing to get her to the lifeboat.

"Several women pulled her up, back into the boat, but a sudden wave swept me further from the boat until I could no longer see it. I heard women yelling for me, but my strength was ebbing and I could not swim back. I suddenly felt a calm. I let myself slide beneath the water and I died.

"Once my spirit left my body, I could see what was going on and eventually a ship came and rescued many survivors. My mother was one, and I was so glad I could save her, even at the cost of my life. I think God rewarded me for my bravery and I have been able to save many more people since that day so long ago." She sat back down.

27

The hunters were speechless, but they gave her a thunderous round of applause, as humans would do in celebration.

"Okay, folks, I don't have anything more," George announced. "However, as you recall, I had you turn on the stopwatches on your phones. I want you to look at your phones as soon as I finish speaking, so you can see how much time has actually passed. I work on dual time, friends; human time and God time. Please write down how much time you think has passed by." When they finished, he said, "Would you please bow your heads and say The Lord's Prayer with me and then look at your watches."

They spoke the prayer and when they opened their eyes, George, Hannah, and Christian were gone. The restaurant became a hubbub of activity again, and only four seconds had passed since everyone was frozen.

Before they left, they shared their times and their guesses varied between one hour and one and a half hours. They were all flabbergasted, but they now understood dual time.

Clay and Lynn Reppert

Wilmington, North Carolina
July 11th, 2016

1

Clay Reppert scratched his head. He knew he dropped his wallet on the floor; he was reaching down to pick it up, his eyes locked on the prize, and in a microsecond, it was gone. A waitress had just walked by, so he took a look under the table and the chair, but it just disappeared and he could not understand it.

His wife, Lynn, tapped him on the shoulder and said, "What are you looking for, Dear?"

Replying over his shoulder he said, "I dropped my wallet just a second ago, and now I can't find it."

She saw it lying on the table and placed her hand on his shoulder. He was beginning to get more forgetful lately and she was worried. "It's right here on the table, Clay. You must have just thought you dropped it."

He sat up and saw it on the table beside his plate. He was absolutely certain he dropped it. Could someone have picked it up and placed it on the table in that short a period of time? He recalled an episode of *The Twilight Zone* where someone could stop time. He Googled it on his phone and came up with the title, *A Kind Of A Stopwatch.* His creative mind was hard at work, so he decided he would put the wallet in a plastic bag and take it to the Wilmington Police Department to have it dusted for prints.

"Lynn, I have to tell you something later, but right now, I want you to watch my wallet and don't touch it, please. I have to get something from my kit in the trunk of the car."

"Okay, Honey."

When he got up from the table, she began to cry. She thought his memory was getting worse, but she continued to humor him. He would be able to retire from the FBI in six months and she wanted him to make it to that time. His boss kept his eye on him too because Clay and Lynn were good friends.

2

Clay opened the trunk and grabbed some plastic bags. He was beginning to get a slight headache courtesy of a small piece of shrapnel lodged in his brain since Vietnam in 1972. He knew he was living on borrowed time, but, he continued to live a relatively normal life. He had done some crazy things in his day. He had a passion for writing science fiction short stories. To date he had over four hundred stories completed, but he didn't have the courage to publish them. Perhaps if there *were* someone else's fingerprints on his wallet, he would seek a publisher, or even self-publish his stories. He had decided that when he retired in six months, he and Lynn would travel to all the places they wanted to see in their lifetimes and the list was long. He closed the trunk and went back inside, seeing the paraplegic man and the woman with one prosthetic arm coming down the stairs. They had grave looks on their faces and he wondered why, since they had been seated with a large group of people. The strange thing about that though was that the group was only seated for about a half an hour before they left. He nodded as he walked past them.

3

A young man dressed in biker shorts, a tank top, and sneakers, with no socks, had been sitting near the front of the restaurant. Although he appeared frozen, like everyone else in the restaurant, he simply willed himself to not move, and since he was facing the table the group was seated at, he was able to watch them through unmoving eyes. He was surprised that God and his children did not realize that he was there, and he thought that perhaps he was becoming more powerful than the so-called Almighty. He laughed inside but remained absolutely motionless. He was slightly concerned when one of the people at the table, Rick Conlen, walked around the human statues as he worked his way to the restroom, staring at him hard and long as he passed by.

Known around these parts as Linde Harmon, Satan was preparing to take on God and his small army tomorrow on the battleship. He controlled eleven werewolves, three witches and a large number of spirits, figuring to give God a hell of a battle. Pun intended he thought, once again laughing inside.

He loved seeing the quizzical looks on the faces of God's minions as they stared at their stopwatches, seeing that only seconds had passed instead of the one hour and nine minutes of God's dual time. Humans were so scatter-brained sometimes and easy to confuse. He decided it was time to go, so he stood up and stepped away from the table, colliding with an older man, coming into the restaurant.

Linde gave the man a shove and said, "Watch where you're going, old man. You almost knocked me over."

"I'm so sorry, Sir," Clay offered in apology, but as he did, he saw something in the younger man's eyes that scared the bejesus out of him.

He stood there and watched the man pay his bill, and when he stepped outside, Clay used a napkin and picked up the man's fork and glass. Perhaps he could lift prints from them and find out who that person was. Something weird was definitely going on in the restaurant, and Clay was going to find out what it was.

4

Hy and Susan ran back to the Inn and raced back upstairs to Steve and Mary's apartment. When they walked into the living room, they saw a brown box on the floor, and they were anxious to see what kinds of weapons they would be using tomorrow to kill werewolves, witches and ghosts. However, they might not make it to the battleship if Adam, Eve and Jamal confronted them on this property. They did not want anything happening to the Wrights nor any of the guests, so they figured they should be outside when the evil trio arrived.

The Witches

Southport
July 11th, 2016

1

After a great night's sleep and a wonderful breakfast at the Wingate Hotel, the four witches drove into town. They walked around for a bit, checking out several of the old trees nearby. They visited the Old Indian Trail Tree. Nearly 800 years old, it was a tree they first visited four-hundred years ago. Still impressive, the tree was a popular spot for visitors to take pictures. The second tree they wanted to see again was the one outside the Live Oak Café. The age of the tree was not known for sure, but it was estimated to be over four-hundred years old.

Finally they made their way to the tree known as the Four Sisters, because four separate trunks grew out of one base. Nobody really knew how old the tree was, except for the witches. It had been planted many hundreds of years ago, but few people knew that there were once seven different trunks growing from the base.

In order to reawaken their powers to be stronger than ever, the sisters had to stand inside the center of the trees, with their backs against each trunk, as they held hands. Every time they had come here, the time frame for the reawakening was never a set amount of time, and there was usually a strange occurrence during the silent ceremony.

One hundred years ago, there was lightning and thunder, but no rain. The weather event only lasted a few minutes, but each trunk of the tree was struck, sending energy into the sisters' bodies.

What would happen this time would remain a total mystery until they joined hands.

2

George, Hannah, and Christian stood a short distance away from the tree; however, they were camouflaged so the witches would not see them. Although George was not overly pleased with the existence of witches, these four could be instrumental in destroying the evil ones tomorrow on the battleship. When he saw them finally join hands, he stretched his hands toward the foursome and then raised them above his head.

The sky turned completely black, but the sisters were bathed in a glow of pure white light. The Heavenly trio watched the witches writhe and wriggle as the energy from the light was absorbed by their bodies.

Less than a minute later, George dropped his hands to his sides and sunlight washed over the landscape again. A moment later the trio were gone.

3

Lucinda shook her arms; they were still tingling from the experience and she was beginning to feel out-of-sorts, almost like she was human again. She looked at her sisters, and they appeared to be undergoing unusual feelings, as well.

When the energy passed through them, the sisters felt stronger than ever. The entire ceremony just seemed so different than the previous ones and they would have to talk it over, sharing their individual thoughts.

"Sisters, are you all feeling very odd right now? My arms are tingling and I almost feel human."

Eliese replied first. "Yes, Lucinda, I am feeling extremely uncomfortable. My stomach is quite upset, like I ate toxic food and my teeth hurt like mad. I can feel something like electric shocks passing though all my limbs, too."

"My joints are killing me," Amanda offered, "I've run marathons and have never felt like this before. What the hell is going on, Lucinda?"

"Guys, look at me!" Janelle exclaimed.

When they looked at her, they were astonished. For the first time in four hundred years, their youngest sister now had eyes, and her face was perfect. She looked amazing.

"Ladies," Lucinda said, "if we weren't witches, I would say we were bewitched. I'm going to go out on a limb here, but I think God has had something to do with this and He must need us to help Him with something really big. Loco Jo's will be open very shortly. That is another strange thing, sisters. The Reawakening apparently lasted for a couple of hours, and that had never happened before.

4

They stepped into the bar and quickly found a seat. Two men and a woman were seated at the bar, and a young couple was seated at a nearby table. They were in animated conversation, so Lucinda cast a listening spell to eavesdrop on their whispered conversation.

"Denise, I don't know about you, but the mission that God wants us to undertake could result in a bunch of dead people. How are we going to destroy eleven werewolves, Lord knows how many spirits, and three witches. This is insane."

The sisters' ears perked up hearing about the three witches, obviously their sisters, too, and they knew they had to find out more about this mission. Perhaps God needed their assistance to eradicate the evil these humans were soon going to face. Prior to the Reawakening, they knew God was powerful but He had never interceded in their lives before today. It would be difficult for Christians to believe that witches would assist God in a mission, but that is what was about to happen.

"I agree, Rick, but look at all the miracles God has performed, getting us together to eradicate malicious entities. The eight people we met this morning had life-changing occurrences bringing them together to disperse the earthbound spirits two years ago. Hy and Susan lost limbs because of what they did to eradicate werewolves from Bethlehem. You regained your sight because God wanted you to see. When we face the paranormal presences tomorrow on the North Carolina, we must prevail and destroy all the malevolence they will use to fight us. I'm ready to head home to see what weapons God has given us to use."

The couple paid their checks and strolled from the bar, hand in hand.

When the waitress checked to see if the four women needed anything, Lucinda inquired. "The couple that just left looked so familiar to me, but I can't put names to the faces. Do you know them?"

"I sure do, Miss. Rick Conlen is a formerly blind lawyer who mysteriously regained his sight. He is also a ghost whisperer. His wife, Denise, used to tend bar at The Pharmacy, but she is studying to become a paralegal so she can work with him all the time. They've been involved in a couple of weird experiences over the past few years, and they are local heroes to us."

"Thank you," Lucinda looked at her nametag, "Shirley. They must just resemble a couple I met some time ago."

When the waitress was out of earshot, the sisters began whispering among themselves, deciding they had to go to the battleship tomorrow and see to it that their evil sisters did not make it out alive.

Clay And Lynn

Wilmington, NC
July 11th, 2016

1

On their way to the city, a brief rain shower slowed Clay down slightly. He learned to be extra cautious in bad weather because when he was a teenager, he had a 1967 Camaro Rally Sport that he loved to death, but he drove like a bat out of hell far too many times. On a dismal April day, when he was heading toward his girlfriend's house, he hydroplaned and ripped the right side of his car to shreds on a guardrail. It cost him almost as much to repair it as the purchase price when he bought the three-year old vehicle. However, when the weather was nice, to the dismay of Lynn, he still drove too fast, until she'd yell at him to slow down.

When they arrived in Wilmington, Clay dropped Lynn off at the Cotton Exchange where she could shop for a couple of hours until he finished his business. He drove to the police station, parked his car, and went inside.

At the information desk, he introduced himself, showed his ID and was then escorted to the fingerprint division. He handed the officer on duty, Mary Jane Thompson, the items he brought.

He explained why he had brought these items and although Officer Thompson was skeptical she kept her professional demeanor and logged the items in, giving Clay a receipt.

"I really need the results as quickly as possible, Officer Thompson. Something strange is going on and if I at least find out who picked up my wallet, I can talk to the person and hopefully, get some information. The fork and the knife were used by a young man who gave me the chills when I ran into him. I don't know how he is involved, but my gut tells me I need to have him identified fast."

"Agent Reppert, I'll see what I can do. I can't make promises but fortunately there is not a lot being processed right now, so you have a chance to get the results later today." She smiled politely, but after he left, she laughed loudly and then took the items to the lab.

2

Clay drove to the Cotton Exchange and drove around the parking lot twice, but every spot was taken. He got a little pissed when he saw a new Beamer taking up two spots, and he had an unprofessional urge to key it, but figured he'd get caught. He wound up parking three blocks away, so he took some time to grab a beer at the Front Street Brewery. The place was packed, and many of the customers at the bar were of the sipping crowd, probably just getting out of the heat for a short length of time before returning to their daily grinds. He noticed a group of men sitting next to each other and figured they might be husbands killing time until their wives' shopping excursions ended.

When a bar server was free, she came over to him, smiled, and said, "Hi, I'm Kay LaMotte. How can I help you today?"

"I think I'd like a beer. What would you recommend, Kay?"

"My favorite is the Dram Tree Scottish Ale. Would you like a taste?"

"That would be great. Thanks."

He watched her walk away and nodded. She was a very pretty young woman and she sported a damn fine body. He had seen her wedding ring and wondered what her husband would be like. He'd been looking for a young couple to create characters for a new short story, and she would certainly fit the bill. Lynn would probably be shopping for at least another hour, so he decided to question her. He watched her head back to him and saw she had a small tattoo of a ship just above her right breast.

She set the small glass of beer in front of him and he sipped it, enjoying the flavor. "This is really good. I would like a large glass of it please."

When she returned with his beer, he inquired about her tattoo.

"This is the battleship North Carolina. It's a museum on the river not too far from here and my husband, Drew, is a member of the crew right now. His grandfather served aboard the ship during WWII and survived all the battles she participated in. The hubby has one too, because grandad passed on a couple of years ago and we wanted to honor his memory by putting his ship on our bodies. Pretty stupid idea, wasn't it?"

"Nah, I'm a 'Nam vet and I've seen some really outrageous tats that guys got when they were hammered. Were you and Drew smashed when you got them?"

"Thanks for your service, Sir. Nope, we were sober as judges."

"My name is Clay." He took a long pull of the beer. "Wow, really good when you take more than a sip."

"Glad you like it. Did you make it home okay?"

"Yeah, except for a small piece of shrapnel in my brain which will eventually kill me. I live life one day at a time and hope for a lot more before I cash in. I've never been on the ship. Perhaps I should check it out tomorrow."

She wiped off an area of the bar and rinsed some glasses while he talked. "Well, tomorrow is no good. It's going to be closed for a special event, but Drew has no clue what's going on. Nobody seems to know. They got the word today that all crew must be off the ship and on this side of the river until further notice. So, I guess we'll have a day together, since I am off. He'll be happy to spend time with his BK. First time he called me that I thought he was referencing one of the whoppers at Burger King, but he says it means 'beautiful Kay'. Funny thing is since that day we've never gone back to Burger King, so I'm always going to wonder." She laughed loudly, garnering the attention of a couple of customers at the bar.

Clay, the FBI agent, was curious. "Has this ever happened before?'

"Not that I know of. There are special events from time to time, but we all know what the event is about well before hand, and most times people are allowed on the ship. As far as I know, a river cruise boat is going to take an entourage over to the ship and then it must immediately return to the dock. Damndest thing anyone around here ever heard. So what does Clay do when he's not in Wilmington drinking beer and hitting on young, married women," she said, mischievously.

"No way, BK. A gal your age would definitely kill me. It would be a nice way to go, but I'm sticking with my wife. I am an FBI agent out of Charlotte, here on vacation, although it could turn into a working vacation very soon."

3

Lynn Reppert was having a great time shopping. She ran into an old friend she hadn't seen in about a decade, so they walked to Port City Java to have lunch and talk over old times. The restaurant was only a couple of doors up from where Clay was having a beer.

The women set their shopping bags at a table by the front window and strolled up to the counter to place their orders. After ordering they returned to their seats carrying steaming cups of coffee and sat down. Foot traffic outside the window was increasing as the morning wore on, but vehicle traffic was moderate. Lynn smiled because quite a few people were carrying packages; there were no economic issues here, she thought.

Her friend, Marcia Logan was also looking out the window at the crowd outside while sipping her coffee. She was having difficulty finding things to say to Lynn since they had been out of touch for so long. Marcia was living the dream as an actress. In fact, she was here working on the pilot for a new TV show about an FBI agent with a super power, but she didn't know if Lynn's husband was still in the FBI. If he was, he was making a pittance compared to what Marcia was going to receive per episode. She could make as much in one year as Clay had made in a lifetime of doing real law enforcement work. She didn't know how Lynn would handle it, so she hesitated telling her old friend what she was doing now.

The silence was lasting much too long, so Lynn finally broke the ice for the second time in the hour they had been together. "Are you here working, Marcia, or something else? Last I knew you were living in California, in a freakin' mansion with servants, maids and the whole damn enchilada. Not too shabby for a small town girl."

She smiled. "I'm working on a new project, but I really can't talk about it too much because it's a pilot. A lot of the indoor stuff is in the can, but now we have to shoot the outside location scenes. I think we'll be here for about three weeks and then back to the west coast. Hopefully the show will be picked up and come on in the fall of 2017. How's Clay doing?"

Lynn debated how much she wanted to tell her about what was going on lately, but she mulled it over, knowing she had to have someone share her burden. She decided to bare her soul.

4

Two guys in navy uniforms stepped into the brewery, laughing like crazy. Of course, their behavior drew the attention of a bunch of customers. Clay and Kay were two of them.

"Hey, Drew and Tank, what the hell are you two doing here in the middle of a work day? Playing hooky, are we?" Kay loudly inquired. "Clay these two are my husband and our friend Tank Lincoln."

They sat down beside Clay. Drew leaned over the bar and gave his wife a kiss, while his friend Tank, ogled her boobs, licking his chops. Clay had to stifle a laugh when he saw that. Kay introduced them to Clay. Tank was damn near as big as his name implied. He was about two-hundred and thirty pounds of solid muscle, his large biceps stretching his shirt sleeves tight.

When they shook hands, Clay felt like his hand was inside a vise until Tank loosened his grip pressure. "Sorry, Clay, sometimes I forget to go a little easy on that. Hope I didn't hurt you."

"Nah, I can take a vise-like grip, as long as it doesn't last more than two seconds. Jeez, you are freaking strong. What do you do for Sammy?"

"You must be a vet. I never hear civilians call the military, Sammy. 'Nam?"

Clay nodded and told him the story.

"Good luck with that, man. If I was a walking time bomb, I'd freak out. I'm a mechanic on the battleship. I'm also a body-builder. My wife has won a bunch of awards for body-building and I'm trying to catch her. Got a long way to go, I'm afraid."

"So, guys, why the hell are you here and not on the ship?" Kay asked, as she brought a couple of beers to them.

"Don't know, Honey," Drew replied. "We were all told to leave the ship and that we need not come back until Wednesday. I know there's something going on tomorrow, but there were a lot of disappointed kids and adults when we had to shut down today."

"Has this ever happened before?" Clay posed the question to both sailors

Both shook their heads. "I've never had this happen, Drew, Have you?" Tank inquired.

"No, I haven't either. I assume it must be something really big, though. I guess we'll find out tomorrow.

Clay finished his beer, and was ready to call the police station, when his phone rang. Not wanting to talk in front of everyone, he excused himself and stepped outside, nearly knocking down an old man. He stared at him and said, "You look like George Burns."

"Yes, I know. I get that all the time. Perhaps you should answer your phone. It could be good news."

He said. "Hello," and when he looked for the old man, he was gone.

5

At the cafe, Lynn was in animated conversation with Marcia about what happened in the restaurant.

"...so, he put the wallet, a fork, and a glass in plastic bags and we came here. He took off, and I don't know where he went, but it seems like he wanted to get the items dusted for prints. Crazy, huh.

"For years he's been writing these outrageous stories, but I tell you, Marcia, they are really good. They're written almost as though he was a character in his tales. The settings are fantastic and the dialogue is so realistic. It scares me that they are this good, because I dug up some stuff he wrote before he was wounded and all the stories are pure crap. He has never had any professional training in literature and he wasn't the brightest light in college. I just can't figure it out. What do you think?"

"Well, you have brought up some interesting points to ponder. Maybe you should be like Tabby King and send Clay's stuff to a publisher, like she did with *Carrie*. Look what happened with her husband. Richard Bachman finally became Stephen King."

Lynn nodded and smiled. "I forgot about that. He'd bust at the seams if any of his stories would be bought by anyone. I just might give that a shot."

She looked out the window and saw Clay running down the street, so she quickly raced outside to see where he was going. She saw him hop in the car and take off, and she immediately called him, but after going to voicemail, she left a message.

6

Clay bounded into the station and was escorted back to the fingerprint division where he once again was met by Mary Jane Thompson.

"Detective, I have good news and strange news. The prints on the wallet belong to an attorney in Southport, named Richard Conlen. We tested the glass and the fork, and found that the DNA was impossible to read, almost as though there were strands from many different people. The three prints we were able to lift from the fork and the glass were all different. I can't figure that out to save my life..."

"How can that be? I've never heard of anything like that in my career. So you're saying that the saliva is a mixture of DNA from an unknown number of people and the prints are from three individuals. Does that about sum it up?"

"Yeah Detective, it does. But the even stranger thing is that the prints belong to people long dead. I imagine we'd find the same thing with the DNA. I'm not going to report this outside of my immediate supervisors, because we'd wind up being a laughing stock in this city."

"I agree with that. I'm going to pick up my wife and head to Southport. Maybe Mr. Conlen could shed some light on this story. Thanks for your assistance, Mary Jane."

"You're welcome, Clay. Let me know what you find out if you can."

Southport, North Carolina
July 11th, 2016

1

Rick, Denise and Walter were in animated conversation when the door opened and Clay rushed inside, followed by Lynn.

He saw the ghost and for a moment, he was frightened, but he had a job to do, and adding a ghost to the strange brew that happened today was just adding another shot to the paranormal drink that was being concocted.

Rick abruptly stood up and asked, "May I help you, sir?" perhaps a little too loudly. He saw Denise raise her

114

eyebrows, and Walter floated off to a corner of the office. Apparently the stranger could see the spirit, and Rick didn't know if that would be good or bad.

Lynn saw the ghost too, and she nearly fainted. She composed herself and hurried to her husband's side.

"Yes, you may, Mr. Conlen. I have some questions to ask you. The first is how did your fingerprints wind up on my wallet, when it was only out of my sight for a second or two? I remember seeing you at the Causeway Café this morning with a large group of people." He laid the report on the attorney's desk, waiting for a response.

Rick picked up the single piece of paper and read the results. There was no way he was going to be able to lie to this guy-Clay Reppert, an FBI agent-but the story he had to tell him was so absurd, he doubted if the agent would believe it. Of course, he and the woman saw Walter, so that might ease what Rick would tell them. "Agent Reppert and, I'm sorry, what is your name?" he asked the woman.

"I'm Clay's wife, Lynn. That ghost is freaking me out, Mr. Conlen. Must it be here?"

"Yes, Mrs. Reppert. Walter Marchant was his name in life. He just told me something very important, something I will need to tell my friends before tomorrow."

"Yeah, what is going on tomorrow, Mr. Conlen? I heard today that the battleship is closed to visitors. Does your group have anything to do with its closing?" Clay asked.

"It does, and please call me Rick."

"I'm Clay and my wife is Lynn. I have a feeling you're going to take us on a verbal rollercoaster here today."

"I am. Please take seats. My wife, Denise, will make some coffee and I think there might be some doughnuts, too. It's going to take some time to fill you in on everything, and I also have a video to show you, as well. Walter was hanging out at the Causeway when we were having our meeting and he saw someone who scared the living shit out of him. Yeah, right, Conlen, living shit. That's a good one. Walter told us that there was a young man in the restaurant, wearing a biking outfit. I stared at him when I went to the bathroom. That's when I saw your wallet on the floor and picked it up, so the waitress wouldn't step on it and possibly drop her tray of breakfasts. Walter swears that it was old Lucifer himself in earthly disguise. I believe him."

Clay laid another sheet of paper on the table. "That guy nearly knocked me over when I came back into the restaurant after getting some latex gloves and plastic bags from my car. His eyes were really creepy, so I picked up his glass and fork and had them tested, too."

Rick read that report, his eyes growing large. "I guess Walter is one hundred percent right. The guy had fingerprints belonging to three dead people, and his DNA was that of many people. I must assume that God, His angel, nor His Son, realized that Satan was present."

Clay and Lynn cocked their heads at the mention of a Holy trio, and leaned forward to hear all about them.

2

Two hours, several cups of coffee, and a bunch of doughnuts later, Rick told them about the phone call from Taylor Halloran and they all watched the video that he had shot at the World Trade Center Memorial.

While they watched the scenes on the wall, blinking very seldom, Rick studied Clay's and Lynn's reactions; that went from disbelief to pure awe.

Lynn saw hundreds, or perhaps, thousands of spirits rise in flight from the deep WTC footprints, and then gasped as she watched scenes of presidential assassinations, the

116

battle of the Alamo, and the planes hitting the towers, screaming at the carnage that she witnessed. There were also scenes of earthquakes, tornadoes and hurricanes. Lynn was mesmerized seeing planes and ships disappearing in the Bermuda Triangle, trying to comprehend where they went. Finally watching the video became overwhelming and she cried her heart out.

Lynn stood up, stepped to her husband, leaned down and kissed and hugged him. She whispered, "I'll never again think you crazy after hearing and seeing all this. I'm not even troubled by Walter any more. You know we have to help these people in the fight tomorrow."

He nodded. "Rick, Lynn and I are in and we'll do whatever we can to destroy the evil that we will face tomorrow. I was a good soldier in my youth and I think I could do it one more time. I hope you'll have us."

Rick was ready to say yes when George, Hannah and Christian entered the office.

3

"Nice outfit, George", Rick said with a giggle.

He wore a bright lime green suit, pink shirt, dark green tie and pink shoes. "This is my Alice Cooper suit. I read that he wore something similar on his first trip to England. I really like his music, you know."

Hannah and Christian couldn't help but laugh, and their joy spread to the others in the office, including Walter. George saw the ghost and asked, "How are you today, Walter?"

Walter floated toward him. "I could be a lot better if I didn't have to haunt the earth, God. When the hell are you going to let me go? I've been in this state too freaking long to suit myself."

117

"In due time, my friend, in due time." George waved his hand, the unlit cigar between his fingers, and Walter vanished.

Lynn said, "Didn't we see you three at the Causeway Café earlier?"

"Indeed you did, my child. I was very impressed with Clay figuring out something strange was going on. I doubt if many people would have questioned the experience, perhaps chalking it up to a little memory loss. You were marvelous, Sir. Of course I did pitch in a little at the fingerprinting unit at the police department. Sometimes the bureaucracy is a tad slow and they require additional help."

"What did you do, God?"

"I think we would all be more comfortable if you all continued to call me George. I sped up the process a bit so you would have the results as soon as you did. Your head injury during the war could have been much worse, but I intervened slightly. I needed you alive for this mission."

Clay was absolutely stunned. He prayed a lot during the war, remembering saying many times, 'God, if you get me out of here alive, I'll be your servant forever'.

Reading his thoughts, George said, "It's okay, Clay, I wish I had a dollar for every man and woman in combat, or other near-death experiences who prayed that. I'd be a rich man, my friend. Of course, I decided I'd take you up on that someday, and now the day is upon us."

The old soldier spent an extraordinary amount of time processing George's words, as he listened to the discussion occurring between the Holy trio, Denise, Rick and Lynn. As his mind churned, he was still able to understand every word that was said, but he only listened, not participating until he heard Rick say, "Satan was in the restaurant with us all this morning, George."

4

First Rick, and then Clay, told the trio about the young man in biker clothes, and as George listened intently, he sat down; his legs were a little shaky.

"This is the first time he was in my presence and I could not feel or see him. I'm afraid he is becoming stronger as more people turn away from religion. However, now that I know he will be on the ship, my children and I will be more prepared.

"I suggest that you all head back to where you are staying and get some rest because we are going to be quite busy tomorrow. There will be weapons in your room, Clay and Lynn, and you'll know how to handle them when you need to. Earlier, I put some God power to work on the four good witches. They will be aboard the ship to help us fight their evil sisters.

"I don't know if everyone will make it off the North Carolina unscathed, because humans don't always do what I think they should do. I gave everyone free will and you must make the best decisions you can make in the fight."

He and His children turned around without another word and walked through the door and into the street. The four humans remained and took some time to discuss the upcoming battle before Clay and Lynn headed back to Wilmington.

The Werewolves

Wilmington, North Carolina
July 11th, 2016

1

Jeff, Vicky and Malcolm were spending time with the 'children', now, fully-grown werewolves.

"I still can't believe I gave birth to all of these wolves, Jeff!" Vicky exclaimed.

He nodded, watching Malcolm brushing them down. "They are magnificent creatures, but my question is what are we going to do with them? We certainly can't keep them in this house forever, and we sure as hell can't turn them loose in the city. They'd go on a killing spree, and I feel that the police would be at our door not too long after the first killing."

"Jeff, there is no way the cops can tie the wolves to us," Malcolm offered as he gave the largest wolf a belly rub.

"I think he's right," Vicky added. The doctor's house was destroyed and nobody saw us leave there with a van full of werewolves. But, I do agree, we still can't let them out to terrorize an unsuspecting city full of people. We need to figure out some options, and then we have to get out of here ourselves."

Jeff nodded. "I agree with that wholeheartedly." He went back to watching Malcolm having fun with the wolves.

2

Unbeknownst to them, during the time they were still in Dr. Little's house, a car was parked on the street, just out of their view.

Blogger, Delroy Addison, saw the van pull away, and a moment later, the place burst into flame. He followed them at a discreet distance and even in the darkness he saw about a dozen large figures enter a house from a side door. Delroy took his iPhone out and tried to get some pictures, but with the flash off, he couldn't determine what the images were. He decided he would remain in his car as long as he had to, hoping to find out what he had actually seen.

During his stake-out, he saw the news on Google about the home burning completely to the ground and firemen could not even find any bodies. The heat was so intense, even the metal file cabinets were melted globs of steel. A spokesman said that they had never seen anything like it before and it might take weeks to find out what caused the conflagration.

3

At 10:03 AM, three people hurried outside and jumped into the van. A smoke screen of burning oil followed the vehicle as it sped away, offering Delroy an opportunity to snoop around. He figured with the way they tore out of there, the threesome had some emergency to attend to, and he might have ample time to see who or what else might be in the house. He first checked the trash cans. When he opened one, a stench unlike anything he had ever smelled before assailed his nostrils and he quickly placed the lid back on top.

He strolled to the back door and tried it, but it was locked. He peered into the basement windows and saw nothing, but he heard sounds: something had to be in that cellar. He needed to get inside somehow. As he worked his way around the back of the house, he saw a window opened just a crack. It was a little high to reach and he couldn't get in. Looking around, he spotted a wooden crate and when he stood on it, he smiled because it held his weight. Dragging it to the back of the house, he placed it beneath the window and stepped up. The window opened easily and he was able to shinny up the wall and slide inside.

There was an odor present, like numerous dogs lived here. Not knowing what breeds he might find, he grabbed a baseball bat that was beside the back door and slowly searched the rooms. When he finished the first floor, seeing piles of dog poop, but no dogs, he took the stairs stealthily and checked out the bedrooms one at a time. One room had a lot of computer equipment, and he wondered why a household would need so much.

Delroy took a bunch of pictures, but he couldn't open up any of the three computers. Medical books, especially about animals, filled a small bookcase. He also took photos of them.

He hurried back downstairs and walked to the inside basement door, hesitantly putting his hand on the knob and opening it a crack. The odor of dogs wafted up the stairs, slamming into his face and he suddenly became afraid.

The door burst open, knocking him over. Standing over him were three large, hideous looking wolves. His eyes grew wide, but he never got a chance to scream before he was torn to shreds.

Wrightsville Beach, North Carolina
July 11th, 2016

1

Sherrl Wilhide sat on the second floor porch, drinking coffee and watching the traffic pass by. She was so relaxed being here with her friends. They were inside taking a little nap after their adventure this morning.

They told her about their breakfast meeting with the Heavenly trio and the ghost hunters, and Sherrl clung to every word they said. She didn't know why she didn't get an invitation, especially since she had already killed a werewolf.

Her life had changed so much after that scary time. She had a number of dates with some wonderful men, and she was a superstar at The Brass Rail where she waited tables. Everyone wanted to sit in her section, and if they couldn't, she at least tried to say hello to as many people as she could. The adoration had died down some, but she still had many, many fans and most of them were very good tippers, too.

Her daydreaming was shattered by the sound of a van crashing into a car in the parking lot below her. Sherrl looked down and recognized the three people who exited the van. Jeff. Vicky, and Malcolm had found where Hy and Susan were staying. She quickly stood up and raced in to tell them who was here.

2

Hyram and Susan stepped out on the porch and looked down into the faces of the three people who had tried to murder them and both of them felt a rage boiling inside, yet they maintained a calm external presence. They didn't want anything to happen to anyone staying here, and hoped that they could talk the threesome out of whatever they were planning. They saw no visible weapons, and that was a good sign, although they had no idea what powers the human werewolves and Malcolm possessed.

They came down the stairs and stood less than four feet away from their enemies. Hyram saw that their van smashed into Laurence's car: he would be really pissed.

"What do you want?" Hy asked in a shaky voice.

"We can't believe that you and your girlfriend made it out of that restaurant alive, Vicky responded, having noted the fear in Lasky's voice. "I have wanted to meet face to face with you two for a long time now and kill you both with my bare hands if possible. You people killed our brethren, and that really pissed me off."

Susan chimed in. "You people aren't even real! You were cloned, for God's sake. How can you even consider yourselves and the wolves we killed as brethren?"

"It's very simple, Miss Mitchell. Perhaps we were cloned from werewolf DNA, but we look, act, and think like humans. We have social security numbers, a home in Wilmington, new identities, and to everyone we know, we are humans in their eyes. Our brethren may not have been human, but we were kin because of the circumstances of our births, for lack of a better term.

"However, discussion of our heritage is not why we have come here. Hyram Lasky was instrumental in the deaths of our brothers and sisters, and he must pay." They began to slowly walk toward the retired cop and the reporter.

3

Sherrl Wilhide was getting strange looks from runners, walkers, and bikers as she headed up Lumina Avenue toward a side street that would bring her out on Waynick Boulevard, just a block east of the Inn. Perhaps it was her PJs that featured images of clowns, and the items she carried in her hands-items she hoped would kill at least one of the people threatening her friends. Since slaying the werewolf, she had really 'grown a pair' and didn't take any shit from anyone.

As she approached the parking lot she heard the women's loud voice, say, "Both of you escaped the explosion but you won't escape now..."

The woman's words were cut off when a silver tipped arrow pierced her heart from the rear and she dropped like a stone, dead.

Sherrl was amazed at how the child size bow and arrow had become adult size. The waitress set another arrow in the bow string and aimed it at the white man. She pulled the arrow back and let it go, but the man turned slightly and the arrow merely pierced the man's side, missing his heart, enraging him.

Sherrl raced toward him while Hyram and Susan went into battle against Malcolm.

4

Laurence Hastings had been reading a novel, enjoying the morning, when he heard a horrible crash on the other side

125

of the old building. He became angry when he heard his car alarm ring out loud and long. Someone must have run into his Bentley. He slowly got up from the wicker chair, as his knees were acting up again. He had to go into his room to get his cane, since he didn't figure he would be walking any distance except to the porch to read.

By the time he traversed the porch and saw the front of a white van mangled together with the right rear of his 'baby', he was totally enraged. Then he saw his three new friends fighting with two men, and a women lay dead on the parking lot with an arrow sticking in her. He had never witnessed anything like this in his life, and he had to help his friends.

He stumbled down the stairs, falling, scraping his hands and hurting his knees, but his adrenaline kicked in, making him feel ten-feet tall and bullet proof. He had to smile in the face of what could be awaiting a man of his age, the Travis Tritt song title ringing in his head. As he joined the fray, menacingly waving his cane like a sword, he also thought of a line from another great country song about not being as good as he was one time, but being as good one time as ever. He hoped he could prove this true.

The ornate cane struck the young black man, opening a gash in his forehead, giving Hyram the opportunity to pin him to the side of the van. Laurence bashed the man one more time, hitting him so hard, the man fell to the ground, unconscious.

Susan and Sherrl were punching and gouging the other man, but he fought back hard, knocking Sherrl into one of the other cars in the parking lot. Laurence saw her shaking her head from the blow she had taken, but Susan was still engaged with the man.

Laurence was at such an angle to him, that the only place he could strike him with the cane would be in the left chest. He swung with all his might and the silver wolf's head broke through flesh and bone, striking the man in the heart, killing him instantly.

Hyram hurried to his car and opened the trunk. He pulled out a set of handcuffs and soon had the young man secured to a door handle on the van.

The two women and the detective smiled at Laurence, thanking him for his assistance, but all he could think about was the damage to his beautiful car.

"Laurence, my friend, don't worry about your car; we'll have it repaired in no time. You don't know what you have done, but you just killed one of the people who tried to kill Susan and me."

"You mean that this man," he looked down at the body, "is Adam, the wolf clone turned human?"

"He sure is, Laurence. You are a hero and will be rewarded for your actions today. There was a large reward for him, and you will be taken care of for the rest of your life." Hyram draped an arm over his shoulders. "Now, I have to call the police to get Jamal, or whatever name he goes by now, into a cell. I have many questions for him. The most important one is to find out where the wolves are?"

Malcolm laughed. "You'll never find out from me, Lasky," he cackled. "Adam's and Eve's 'children' will begin a new reign of terror, like nothing ever seen before."

The other humans felt the chills of fear coursing through their bodies at these words.

5

When Steve and Mary stepped onto the porch, carrying a bottle of wine, glasses and a plate of cheese and crackers, they saw what appeared to be four very exhausted people.

Laurence, Hyram, Susan and Sherrl had already killed two bottles of wine and a six-pack of beer. The owners of the Carolina Temple Island Inn set everything on the coffee table and took their seats on the porch swing.

"Our granddaughter, Molly, called us earlier and told us what was going on, but she was really upset and I don't know if we got the entire story. First of all, are you all okay?" Steve inquired.

They all nodded, but Laurence replied, "The bastards wrecked my car, so I'm going to have to stay a couple of more weeks if you can find room for me."

"We'll figure something out, old friend," Mary replied.

"So what happened today?" Steve asked.

After everyone told their particular stories, with Steve and Mary clinging to every word and hand movement, silence prevailed for only a very short time, seconds, actually.

"I'm sure this goes for Mary, too, but I am amazed with all of you, especially you, Laurence, for getting into it at your advanced state of decay."

Laurence shot him a glance, laughed and said, "Thanks, you bastard."

That broke everyone up and the tension was gone.

"Sherrl, what were you thinking you could do with a child's bow and arrow set?" Mary inquired, picking up the bow and an arrow-both made of plastic.

"Well, I trusted that God provided us with exactly what we would need. When I set the arrow in the bow, they both grew in size and I could see that the arrowhead was now some kind of metal. It was shiny and looked sharp as all hell. I let fly and the arrow corrected itself in flight, driving through the woman's back, piercing her heart, and punching through her chest. She dropped like a rock, deader 'n hell."

That elicited another round of laugher, which also seemed to bring on the hunger and thirst. They polished off the cheese and crackers and the bottle of wine. Susan hurried upstairs to grab another six-pack of beer and a tray of veggies. Mary brought out two more bottles of wine and sliced bologna.

While that was happening, the couple who had not met the heroes from the north, strolled onto the porch; he was wearing a speedo and she a bikini. Laurence, Steve and Hyram stared at her for a long time, and Susan checked out her husband.

"Hi," the man said, "I'm Elliot Ringgold and this is my wife, Lizz, with two zs." Give us a couple of minutes to change and we'll be right out. We can't wait to hear all your stories. We have wine, beer and fruit and will bring that, as well." They headed inside, as the stares continued.

"Well, gang, I think we'll be talking a lot this evening, so let's take a break until Elliot and Lizz with two z's return." Steve said.

6

Hy, Susan, and Sherrl told their stories once again, talking for over an hour, combined. They also had time to drink and eat. While they talked, the mother and daughter from Pittsburgh and the female couple from Kentucky arrived and joined the group.

Lizz and Elliot were mesmerized by the individual tales of heroism and fear. They were listening to Sherrl tell what happened out in the parking lot this morning, and Elliot had a question. "When you shot Jeff, you missed his heart. Why didn't he tear you apart, since he had werewolf strength?"

"Good question, and something I thought about all day. My only conclusion is that the arrow must have sapped his strength. He had broken it off, but the arrowhead was still inside him. I surmise that the silver was still working its magic."

"That makes sense to me, Sherrl. So what happened after that?"

"Well, I had a couple of arrows left, but I figured if I ran as fast as I could toward him, I could knock him to the ground and then he might be not as feisty; so I did. I saw that Susan and Hyram were taking on the black man. Then I saw Laurence stumbling down the steps, carrying a cane with what appeared to be a silver handle."

"That amazes me, Laurence. At your age, you had no reservations about jumping in and helping out your friends," Lizz stated.

Laurence nodded. "Trust me, Lizz, it amazed me too. I think I was more pissed off about my car being damaged then what was actually happening in the parking lot, but that didn't last too long. I saw Adam take a swing at Hyram, but he blocked it with his prosthetic arm. It made an interesting sound, but Hyram seemed unhurt, so I just charged in there as best as I could. Once I was able to get a good swing at him with my cane, everything unfolded so clear in my eyes. I felt the resistance when the wolf's head of my cane hit his chest, and then it pushed through. The sound of it hitting bone was excruciating and then it pierced his heart. Adam only grunted before he fell, and I must admit, it felt good to kill him. I have never killed anything intentionally in my life, but possibly saving my new friends was a rewarding feeling. A few moments afterward, however, I vomited."

"After Adam went down, I moved on to Jamal to help Susan out," Hyram interjected. "She was having a tough time with him, but I managed to knock him unconscious and then I had time to get cuffs from my car. I don't think we'll ever get any information from him about the location of the wolves. At the police station, they couldn't find any known address for him, nor Adam and Eve. The three of them were pretty smart, not carrying any ID, and the plate on the van had been stolen a couple of weeks ago. I imagine we'll face them tomorrow at the battleship."

"Lizz and I wish you all our best tomorrow. Unless we get a call from God, I'll continue to be a non-heroic real estate agent and Lizz a physical therapist."

"Don't get upset about not being included in this fight, guys," Laurence replied. "I haven't been invited to participate either, but I plan to watch from the Riverwalk."

"I do, too," Sherrl said. "I guess Laurence and I did what we were supposed to do. I am totally whipped both physically and mentally, but I, too, will be showing my support from the sidelines tomorrow."

During all this time, there were two clandestine observers. Fred, the squirrel, watched and listened from the branch of a tree beside the porch. Walter was invisible, sitting on the hammock; he would be aboard the North Carolina tomorrow and hoped his actions would garner his exit from this world.

By ten o'clock the porch was deserted.

Witches and Werewolves And Ghosts

Wilmington, North Carolina
Midnight, July 11th, 2016

1

Four witches stood on the Riverwalk, staring at the great battleship across the water. Water slapped the wooden supports, and an occasional fish jumped out of the river, seeking an unseen bug. On both bridges spanning the Cape Fear River, traffic was light, but still created some sound to break the quiet night. The witches watched for movement aboard the North Carolina, but they saw none. It was possible that Christian froze their sisters until tomorrow when the good sisters would have to confront them, and quite possibly kill them. The triplets' evil ways had to end, and if the only way that could be accomplished was by their deaths, that would be the price to pay.

There were still a few people walking across the boards, some of them carrying small boxes of food from restaurants and bars, talking quietly. One young woman uttered some well-chosen profanities after she broke a heel on her shoe. Her escort, a handsome, young man with bright eyes, grabbed her arm to keep her from falling. He eyed the four woman watching him, nodded and smiled.

Moments later, the witches heard the air rustle, and the couple screamed at the top of their lungs; Hundreds of translucent specters filled the sky, seemingly being drawn to the battleship. Though the humans were extremely scared, they could not stop watching the spectacle. The witches noticed that the ghosts were trying desperately to stop from being pulled across the river, but they couldn't.

Now, along with the first sounds, came the sounds of moaning and crying, as the spirits kept attempting to turn around to go back to wherever they had come from.

The young couple, eyes wide with fright, could not move their feet, as though they had been nailed to the boards, and they shivered at the sounds they heard. They seemed to be incapable of doing anything but screaming, until the experience ended about five minutes later. Their motor skills returned and they raced off the boardwalk, onto the street, and into the darkness.

Whoever else could have witnessed the incident, was also gone, and quiet returned for several minutes

The silence was shattered once again by the growling of several animals about a hundred yards away.

2

An hour earlier, in a cell in the Wilmington jail, Malcolm sat on his bunk, with his head resting in his hands, wondering how the hell he would get out of here and back to the wolves.

He heard a noise and turned toward the source, seeing a young man, wearing a bicycler's outfit, hovering in mid-air against the far wall. It looked so ridiculous that Malcolm had to laugh, drawing the attention of a guard.

"What you laughing about, Sonny? There ain't nothing funny about being behind bars."

"Nothing important, officer, sir. I just thought of something funny that happened to me when I was a kid."

The fifty-something, marginally overweight cop smiled. "When you was a kid? You still are a kid. I probably have shoes older than you, and I still wear them. Quiet down and go to sleep." He walked away

"Who the hell are you?" Malcolm asked the man that the guard could not see.

"You're on the right track when you say hell, since that is my domain. You're going to love it when you're a permanent resident." He cackled. "Adam and Eve will be waiting for you. They are evil ones, those two. Of course, you also triggered a bomb, so you must pay when the time comes."

Looking concerned, Malcolm asked, "Am I to die, soon?"

"Not necessarily, but I'm not here to talk about your death, but to give *you* assistance getting out of here. I need you to get back to your house and take your wolves to the battleship. Tomorrow we will go up against God and His followers and I'm looking for a big win on that boat. Three evil witches and a boatload, no pun intended, of ghosts are waiting for us and the wolves. I am so ready to fix that old man's wagon in this showing, and I think we will have plenty of firepower with our small army."

Malcolm was stunned. He was going to go into battle against God. Whoa, this was something he didn't see coming, but he knew he was ready. "Okay, Devil, get me out of here and I'll get the wolves to the ship."

When the guard came back a minute or two later, he dropped his coffee. The cell was empty.

3

Malcolm arrived back at the house, walked around the exterior, and was disturbed to find a window open; he hoped nobody had gotten in because they would probably never get out once the wolves saw them.

He unlocked the kitchen door and stepped inside. Immediately he was assailed by the stench of blood; then he saw what was left of the body on the floor. He saw something under the kitchen table and reached down to grab the digital camera. He looked through the pictures, seeing shots of him and Adam and Eve leaving Doctor Little's office. Surprisingly there were no pics of the pups, but the man took a lot of shots inside the house, catching one shot of a wolf that was about to attack him. Malcolm took the camera card out and put it in his pocket.

When he opened the basement door and looked down the stairs, he saw the wolves milling about, chewing on some of the man's bones. The crunching noises penetrated Malcolm's skull, and he didn't particularly like the sound.

Telepathically, he called them up to the kitchen and escorted them outside and into the van. They just barely fit inside the storage area of the van, and one had to curl up on the front seat beside him to make the trip to the river.

He arrived at the river and opened the back doors of the van. The wolves jumped into the water, some of them growling, and swam toward the battleship. After the last one was aboard, Malcolm hopped back into the van and started it up. He turned on the headlights and four women were standing in front of the van with their arms outstretched, hands held in the stop positions. He was unable to move forward, so he put the gearshift in reverse and tried to back out. Once again, the vehicle would not move. He tried one more time each direction but the truck was frozen in place.

Malcom exited the vehicle and raced toward the river. He dove in and swam toward the ship.

When he was midway across, and thought he was home free, he was pulled downward into the murky depths. A couple of moments later, he popped up from the river, missing his right arm. He screamed as the gator bit into his back and took him under again. The struggle for life only lasted for a short time before Malcolm was dragged to the bottom of the river where his remains were feasted on by the dwellers of the deep.

The witches' jobs were done for the moment, so they decided to go back to the hotel to get a little sleep before the battle would begin.

Witches, Werewolves And Walter

Wilmington, North Carolina
July 12th, 2016

1

Standing at the front of the boat, Clay looked toward the battleship. The hunters were on their way to do battle with God against many paranormal creatures. For sure there were three witches, eleven werewolves and an unknown number of pissed-off ghosts. He wondered if this was the way troops felt as they headed toward the beaches of Japanese-held islands, not knowing how many enemy they would be facing, or if their enemy would even be seen until they wanted to be seen. He silently laughed, knowing that the battleship wouldn't be peppered with shells from Big Mo, or hundreds of planes dropping bombs and napalm. These hunters were on their own, following a God they trusted implicitly. Some of us may die today, but if we don't rid the world of these creatures, we will let a whole lot of people down, he thought.

He snuck out of the hotel early this morning, after spiking Lynn's evening cocktail with a couple of Ambien so she wouldn't know he was gone. He didn't want her on the ship, but he did, however, write a note to her in case he didn't return, and he kissed her on the cheek before leaving the hotel. Clay stopped for a cup of coffee and the doughnut he was not supposed to eat, and drove down to the Riverwalk, where he met up with most of the hunters. He explained how he learned about today's battle and that he wanted to help.

One of the hunters, Kyle, offered him a squirt gun, but Clay showed him his. "Welcome to the club, Clay. There is danger, but squirting ghosts is a blast."

Clay nodded and smiled, but he had seen that enthusiasm too often in Vietnam, and some of those guys got killed; they had the John Wayne complex, figuring they could whip the enemy all by themselves. He made a mental note to keep an eye on Kyle today. Perhaps Kyle had forgotten what put him in a wheelchair in the first place.

2

Rick and Denise Conlen leaned over the side of the boat, staring at the ship where they had battled ghosts two years ago. The memories flooded back to them, and they became afraid again.

3

Promptly at 8 AM, on July 14th, 2014, they stood on the wooden sidewalk looking across the Cape Fear River at the great old battleship. The North Carolina had seen a lot of action in its day. As the first newly built battleship put into service in World War II, she saw action in every major engagement in the Pacific theater. She served with distinction for over six years, and in 1962, she was turned into a museum.

Through the special glasses, they stared at her for a lengthy time, seeing figures scurrying around on the deck, on top of the superstructure and sitting on guns and the airplane's wings. Some waved, while others cupped their hands around their mouths, probably trying to antagonize those who would soon be aboard her, ridding her forever of spirits.

Rick heard a lot about her over the time he'd lived in Southport and it was reported that there were only two spirits haunting the ship; one malevolent and one peaceful and shy. He certainly knew that someone was feeding the general public a crap sandwich, probably to keep people coming. He figured if he was a visitor and heard there were only two spirits on board, he could deal with it. Already Rick counted nine ghosts and he figured there were many more in the bowels of the ship. And then again, perhaps visitors were given that information because only two had ever been seen.

A couple of minutes later, Hannah arrived and everyone turned toward her, hoping to hear that this was all a joke and they could all go home.

She smiled at them and then said. "Thank you all for coming. As you all saw, there are many more than two spirits on board the North Carolina. They have learned the art of hiding, sometimes in plain sight, but you should be able to send them all on their way in a short period of time. Does everyone have a squirt gun, a bottle of water and a pair of glasses, and do you have each other's cell phone numbers?"

They all nodded, but Bernadette raised her hand. "I'm sure you're going to tell us the purpose of these items, but may I venture a guess?"

"You certainly may. What do you think these items are for?"

"I think the water that you provided is special and when used to fill the squirt guns, we will be able to shoot them and that action will allow them to shed their earthbound chains and journey to where their final reward awaits. I haven't been able to figure out the glasses, though."

"You are correct. You are each to carry a bottle filled with holy water at all times, in order to refill your squirt guns; the glasses will allow you to see the spirits as though they are flesh and blood.

4

Later, on the battleship, Rick and Denise headed down a number of ladders, the last being a spiral type, and arrived in the section where the big guns' shells were stored. Many were on a conveyer system to be fed upward to the banks of weapons. The pair couldn't even begin to count how many were there on display and how much firepower this battleship had been capable of producing all those years ago. There were hundreds of bags of powder that would be loaded in the breech behind the big shells, and when ignited would propel the round out through the barrel to targets up to many miles away.

Denise's eyes never stopped moving. She felt the hairs on the back of her neck stand up and she was certain a very evil spirit was somewhere in this compartment. As she conducted a visual sweep, she caught the slightest motion of something that had nearly blended in with a white cardboard cutout of a sailor with an arrow sign affixed to the front signifying the direction of the tour. She kept staring at it just to make sure that she wasn't seeing things and moments later she saw a ghostly head peer out from behind the cardboard sailor. She was unwavering as she slowly raised her black squirt gun and then her hand moved swiftly, bringing the weapon to bear on the spirit. She pulled the trigger and held it for a very short time, but time enough to fire four holy water bullets. Three of them found their mark and the spirit dissolved, scowling at her for ending its earthbound existence. The spirt was on its way to Satan's dominion. She felt good with her first 'kill' and knew she would be ready for anything.

Rick saw a spirit darting behind a row of shells lining a wall. He led it with his squirt gun and when he saw an opening, he fired. The jet of water hit the ghost in the right arm and spun him around. He kept running, finally dissolving into a pool of water on the metal floor. Rick smiled knowing he had done a good job sending this spirit to its final reward. He was elated when he saw the vapor was Heaven bound because the spirit looked like a kid, probably no more than eighteen or nineteen when he died.

Denise was still checking out the area and when she heard something behind her, she spun and fired her squirt gun hitting Sammy slightly below the waist.

Sammy looked down where the water bullet hit and saw wetness, but there was no pain, so she deduced that humans couldn't be harmed by the holy water in the squirt guns.

Denise lowered her gun and said, "Oh, Sammy! I'm so sorry. This ship is starting to give me the creeps, and I'll be happy when we are done here. Did you guys run into any ghosts?"

"Yeah, we did. Each of us sent one on its way, one up and one down. How about you and Rick?"

As she saw Rick approaching, she nodded her head. "We each got one and then searched the area thoroughly. Didn't see any more."

"It seems as though we are only allowed to send one spirit on its way. You guys think this is just a test for us to see how well we handle ourselves?" Sam said.

"You might have something there, Sam," Rick replied. "Kyle got one, and we all did, so that leaves Bill,

Aaron and, uh, I'm not sure if Bernie got one, but I'm guessing we can probably head back up and go out on the deck. Unless a couple of ghosts are going to force them to a lower level, my bet is that the remainder of lost souls will be waiting for us topside."

5

Aaron Pammer remembered one ghost he sent on his way to his final reward.

The spirit was probably about five feet eight inches and he wore thick glasses. He opened his mouth and spoke slowly. "I know what you must now do and I accept my fate. There are many of us and few of you, so your work will not be easy. My name is Ron Mazzaro and I was a radio operator during the war on this ship. I died in 1987, almost forty years to the day after the North Carolina was decommissioned. I don't know how my spirit arrived aboard the ship because I was in Connecticut, near my home, keeping watch over my daughter and her husband. I don't know who will watch over them now because soon I will be gone. I hope God knows what he's doing by removing us from earth because I think there is a need for us to remain. That's all I have to say, so do what you must."

Aaron pulled the trigger and watched the spirit dissolve into a small puddle on the chair. Moments later, the puddle turned into vapor and he watched it evaporate in an upward motion, so he figured Ron was on his way to Heaven. Ron's message troubled him somewhat but only for a minute or two

As the boat drew closer to the ship, these words had come back to him. He realized Ron was trying to warn him that he would once again do battle on this ship and they would need as much help as they could get. Aaron was always prepared to die, but he certainly wanted more time on this earth; only time would tell.

6

As the small cruise boat approached the dock on the port side of the ship, in front of the stern, onlookers began to line the Riverwalk, wondering what was going to take place. Many of them knew the battleship was closed for the day, yet a cruise boat docking was enough to whet everyone's curiosity appetite.

The hunters stepped from the boat onto the dock and looked up at the great battleship; it appeared empty, much like the beaches Marines and soldiers invaded during World War II. Many, if not all, of the hunters knew this was a false sense of what was to come. Hundreds, if not thousands of spirits were hiding on board. Adding eleven werewolves and three witches to the mix was going to make the fight very difficult.

Slowly the hunters walked across the dock and up the short flight of stairs. They headed into the deserted information area and gift shop. The silence was spooky, some of them thought, pun intended. They carried their bows and arrows, and squirt guns at the ready; seeing grown people with children's 'weapons' would have been quite laughable if they would have been parading down Main Street, USA. These weapons would become very formidable in a few minutes as they walked up the gangplank to the deck of the battleship. The slight breeze was causing the flags to flap and snap, the only sounds that were heard at the moment.

7

Bernadette was the first to step onto the ship

A moment later, three ghosts appeared in front of her. She aimed her squirt gun at each one, pumping a couple of holy water bullets into their translucent figures. With scowls of hate and howls of agony, each one dissolved into a puddle of water that soon turned to mist. The mist of each ghost began the downward plunge into hell.

8

Several heartbeats later, hundreds of spirits were in the air above the deck of the ship. The hunters trudged on board, spreading out, firing their squirt guns at the nearly invisible figures, dropping many of them, but for every one that was eliminated, two or three took their places. They began to pummel the humans, knocking them over, scaring the living crap out of many of them, even though they had gone through this before.

The twins, Sammy and Sam, along with Bill and Aaron, headed down the narrow stairs to the sleeping area of the ship. They erased twenty to thirty spirits on their way down and when they were in the sleeping quarters, forty to fifty more spirits, some wearing uniforms from all the wars, besieged the four people who were firing holy water bullets as fast as they could.

More spirits came out of nowhere, and had they been solid figures they would have filled a great deal of the space; there were just that many. When a hunter emptied a squirt gun, he or she would fill it from the water bottle and start firing again.

The mist was leaving behind a lot of water and as he charged a handful of the ghosts, Sam slipped and fell on the deck. He struggled as fifteen apparitions smothered him, beginning to choke the air from him.

Sammy rushed toward him, firing her squirt gun, but she didn't think it was going to do the trick. She was certain that they would take her brother's life, so she took her water bottle and swung it back and forth spraying the enemy with a large number of droplets, wiping them out, just as Sam was taking his final breaths.

She quickly administered artificial respiration and brought him back to life, but now her squirt gun was almost empty. She lifted her water bottle seeing it was full and smiled, saying, "Brother, George has given us bottomless bottles of water. I think we'll be okay. Now get your ass up and let's get some more of them.

Bill and Aaron felt they were having a turkey shoot; translucent figures were being whisked away to that happy hunting ground below. When a couple of moments of no shooting occurred, Bill laughed like a hyena.

"What's so funny, Bill?" Aaron asked, as he reloaded his gun.

"If any of us really screw up and wind up in hell, we're going to be screwed. They'll be waiting for us to kick our asses, like we're doing to them now."

"You got that right, my friend, but I'm not going to worry about that now." He had to laugh too as more of the phantoms attacked them again.

9

Back on the upper deck, very close to the bow, the remainder of the hunters were wiping out hordes of specters charging toward the group that was fighting side by side and in a small circle, surrounded by them.

Kyle recalled when he saw the spirits of the Mexican army attacking the Alamo, and this is how the Texans and other Americans fought them off for thirteen days. He kept firing and they kept coming, until he heard a roar above him.

The plane that was circling was the Kingfisher. It was built to scout out enemy aircraft and subs. It was built to be able to manage the wear and tear of traveling on the ship and being launched by catapult.

During World War II, three of these planes were assigned to the North Carolina, along with a staff of twenty-three.

Launching the plane was not an easy task since it had to be catapulted from the deck of the battleship. The apparatus that helped the launching process included a black powder charge to assist getting the plane up to 70 miles per hour. The catapults would also serve to retrieve the planes when they returned.

Kyle, and a few of the others who watched the plane, as they continued to battle the ghosts, saw when it flew over the ship that Christian was piloting the aircraft. Suddenly, they were all drenched as a holy water 'bomb' hit the deck, decimating the translucent soldiers.

Now that that battle was over, the hunters could continue to root out and eliminate the remainder of the spirits. However, they would still have a lot of work on that front.

Sitting in the captain's chair in the conning tower, Satan, still disguised as a human, saw George and Hannah standing on the railing at the bow of the ship. Satan actually thought it resembled a scene from the movie, *Titanic*. He nodded to them and applauded the use of the plane to wipe out hundreds of his evil spirits. The next phase of the battle was about to begin.

10

Lynn Reppert awakened shortly after Clay left. She went to the bathroom, thinking he might be there since he wasn't in bed, and when she didn't see him in the room anywhere, she looked outside and saw the car was gone. She tried to call him on his cell, but it went straight to voicemail. A couple of minutes later, she saw and read the note; then she hurriedly got dressed and headed to the Riverwalk.

She joined a growing crowd of people who were watching people running around on the upper deck of the battleship. Pulling a small pair of binoculars from her purse, she focused in on the people, searching for Clay. Everyone was carrying what appeared to be squirt guns, water bottles and child size bows and arrows. They appeared to be squirting one another, but, no, she saw Clay aim at something that wasn't there. He squeezed the trigger a couple of times and then aimed at something else that wasn't there. She was flabbergasted.

Several minutes later, she saw a plane lift off of its perch and begin flying around the ship. Soon, it flew over the deck and it dropped what appeared to be a very large balloon. The balloon fell near the bow, although she couldn't see what it hit. Not too long after that, the plane retuned to its spot on the ship and a young boy stepped out of the cockpit.

Lynn had no idea what was going on, and then she saw something really freaky as four women hovered above the railing.

11

Catapulting themselves from the other side of the river, the four witches touched down on the deck; and once they did, their sisters were freed from their frozen states. Another battle was about to begin.

With lightning speed, the triplets arrived on the main deck and were faced by nine humans. The men and women fired holy water bullets at them, but they were ineffective. Then they each loaded their bows with an arrow and fired them. The silver tipped arrows passed right through their bodies leaving the mortals aghast; how could they kill witches, they all thought?

The triplets saw their sisters standing behind the men and women, so they shot lightning bolts from their fingers toward both the people and the good witches. When the humans dropped to the deck, the sizzling hot light flashes singed some hair and clothing, and the four witches that were behind them were launched backwards by the power of the bolts.

Recovering quickly, the four sisters returned the favor to the triplets, although their finger lightning wasn't quite as powerful, and the evil sisters batted them away like shooing gnats or flies, cackling as they did so.

The evil witch named Marta took to the sky, grabbing the ship's bell as she passed by, her magic freeing it from its base. She flew a circle over the ship and then hovered thirty feet above the humans who watched her every move. She dropped the heavy bell and it hurtled toward the mortals, who could do nothing but scatter, hoping they wouldn't get hit. The witch watched as the bell hit the deck, gouging out a large section of planking and bouncing away, narrowly missing Clay. He somehow managed to leap out of the way just before it bounced on the space he had just occupied. Marta was not happy, not getting any satisfaction out of that stunt, but she knew she and her sisters would have a lot more to throw at them.

Lucinda moved the bell with her mind and replaced it on its pedestal, and then she bellowed as loud as she could, startling Marta and Giselle. Bella, the other evil witch didn't seem to be affected by the sound waves, so she mentally lifted Lucinda off her feet and tossed her high in the air. The evil witch landed on the crane that would retrieve the planes when they returned to the ship. Lucinda landed hard and fell to the deck, shaken, but unhurt.

The witches began to battle each other with every magic trick they knew until they seemed to have nothing left.

As the battle proceeded, Kyle was trying to think of ways to destroy the evil ones. So many solutions crossed his mind, but were rejected for one reason or another. He finally thought of a plan that could work. He huddled with his fellow hunters and told them his strategy.

They circled the witches and joined hands.

Kyle prayed out loud. "Lord, hear our prayer. We do not want these children of yours to die, for they were once just like most of us, with dreams and goals to look forward to. It is through your grace that we have all we could need or want and it is through your grace that we ask you to drive the demons from the witches known as Giselle, Marta and Bella. Drive them out so these women can become mortal again and live lives in your service."

As Kyle prayed, the others joined in, offering their unique prayers, until all seven witches stopped fighting one another and a calm came over them.

Moments later, the evil witches began to writhe, curse, and scream, as the spirits left their bodies, rising over their heads, staring down at the ones they inhabited for so many centuries. The spirits also glared at the humans, their hands still touching by the fingertips. If just one of them would break the circle, that person would receive the spirits that were free to go anywhere once inside a human host.

Bella shouted out, "People do not break the circle no matter what. The evil spirits will be able to invade anyone once contact is broken. You must keep holding hands and pray with all of your might."

12

The Staunton twins and Bill raced onto the deck from below.

Samantha screamed, "Werewolves are right behind us, and I think Aaron is dead..."She saw her friends in a circle, hands touching. In the center of the circle were seven women, whom she assumed were the witches and hovering above them all were what appeared to be spirits, but they looked different than the ones they had all been fighting since arriving on board. "Who are they?" she asked, pointing at the black entities.

Bernadette responded. "Sammy, these are the spirits that were inside three witches causing them to be evil. We can't break our circle or one or more of us could be facing the possibility of them invading our bodies. We can't help you fight." She bowed her head and started to pray again.

Three werewolves burst from the hatch and were met with arrows released by the three humans. Two arrows found their marks and the werewolves died, screaming and growling. The third wolf was wounded, making it angrier than ever; and it launched itself at Sam, snapping its jaws, but missing the young man.

Sam whirled around and managed to trip the creature. The wolf fell to the deck, landing on the shoulder that was still carrying an arrow. The arrow was pushed deeper, causing the animal more pain and rage.

It stood up and was ready to pounce on Sam when Bill's arrow found its heart, killing it instantly.

As more wolves climbed the stairs and appeared on the deck, Sammy and Sam started firing their squirt guns at the dark spirits. Of the nine, two dissolved. When the witches saw this, they hurried to the circle of humans and grabbed their toy weapons, immediately firing at the spirits, watching one by one dissolve until there were none left.

The hunters were now free to turn their attention to the new threat.

13

When Hyram saw werewolves pouring out from the hatch onto the deck, he began to sweat profusely. His knees got weak, and he thought he would topple over from the fear coursing through him. With the exception of Susan none of the others had ever seen creatures like this. Their yellow eyes were nearly bulging from their sockets, sharp teeth and claws seemed larger than they probably were. Their breath, even at about twenty-five feet away, was horrid. Hy stared at them, his eyes large as well, as they surveyed their dead brothers and sister lying on the deck with arrows sticking out from their chests.

When they saw and smelled their dead brethren, they howled with deep pain and then turned their attention back to the humans who cowered in front of them. The humans were holding bows with arrows at the ready and the wolves became afraid.

Arrows traversed the space between humans and wolves and soon there were primal screams as several of the silver tipped arrows struck flesh and bone; however, only two dropped. The remainder of the wolves attacked by leaping through the space, landing near or on the people trying to kill them.

One wolf landed on top of Hyram and the action also took Susan down with him. Both of them struggled with the strong beast as it lashed out with powerful legs, claws slashing the air just in front of the amputees. Just as the wolf opened its mouth trying to bite Hyram, he lifted his right arm, offering the wolf his prosthetic. The wolf ripped it from his body and as it gnawed on it, the wolf couldn't understand what it was chewing and stopped attacking.

In that short period of time, Susan was able to crawl out from under Hyram and she grabbed an arrow, ramming into the creature's chest, hitting its heart. She pushed with all her might, driving it deeper, feeling the beast's hot breath as it was expelled from its mouth. The wolf looked at her, not with fear or anger, but seemingly with curiosity, wondering how this tiny human female could inflict mortal damage to a werewolf. The animal sighed, closed its eyes and fell to the deck, pinning Hyram until a couple of his friends were able to free him.

The other wolves backed off and leaped about the ship, taking themselves out of harm's way. It would be much harder to kill them now, many of the hunters thought.

14

The hunters planned to sweep the ship's main deck and superstructures in pairs, knowing a wolf could be hiding anywhere, ready to pounce and kill them, so the process was slow and steady. Not only were they up against about six werewolves, there were still an unknown number of spirits that needed to be dispatched.

15

Mandy Fairchild had joined the group on the boat, just before they headed to the battleship. She was greeted warmly by the hunters, as she was the only survivor of the two couples who were camping on Masonboro Island during The Gathering. She was paired with Bill Saunders. Bill's hurt was more recent, losing his friend, Aaron Pammer today, but they shared the common denominator of losing loved ones. Mandy lost her husband Darrell and her friends, Maura and Jason Witson during the battle against the spirits they had to send from the darkness to the light. She didn't know what she was going to do with her life after losing her husband, but when she returned home two years ago, she found out that Darrell's paranormal novel, *Unknown,* was going to be turned into a movie. The process was long and tedious, especially since the author had passed on, but the movie was to be released in fall. If it became a hit, she could find herself quite wealthy. She had taken up Darrell's mantle after finding a half written book on a flash drive. She read the manuscript and decided it needed to be finished, so she worked on it for eight months and the book was published just before last Christmas.

16

Bill remembered the day he met all of these people at a restaurant in Wrightsville Beach.

He was dressed in mismatched, disheveled, visibly dirty clothing. He wore a camouflage sweat soaked baseball cap. His gray beard was matted with vegetation of some kind, and when he smiled, his teeth were obscenely yellow, like those of a long time smoker. Even though he looked and smelled bad, he carried himself tall and proud. He was still about fifteen feet from the table, when he removed his dark sunglasses.

Denise gasped, looking into his incredibly blue eyes. He arrived at the table and stood behind his seat, facing outward. Diners began returning to their seats, and those who had been seated outside, came in. Denise felt that they were in the presence of someone more powerful than they, in the guise of a poor, dirty, old man.

Long moments passed before he raised his hands, palms facing up and with that motion, everyone in the restaurant rose as well.

His voice was soft as a whisper, yet powerful as he spoke. "Father, these people, seated at this table, will soon be instruments in your hands. Through them you will finally have your lost souls freed of their earthly chains. However, the dark one, the black angel, will attempt to keep your children from their reward in your kingdom. These soldiers will need your grace and the strength of many more times their number to complete the task you have commissioned. I ask you to grant them the wisdom, the stamina, and the time they will need to defeat the enemies of Heaven. For through their perseverance, the spirits of those who never had the opportunity to surrender to you, will be able to move on from the darkness to light. May your will be done on earth as it is in your heavenly kingdom. In the name of the Father, the Son and the Holy Spirit. Amen."

He dropped his hands, and everyone took their seats.

He sat down at the table and took a long drink of water, buttered a small piece of bread and ate it slowly, not being interrupted by anyone. When he finished he said, "If you have any questions to ask of me, please do so, because I will not leave your presence until I am satisfied that all your inquiries are answered."

He quietly waited for the first question. He knew what it was going to be, because he heard it many times over the years. He took a sip of water and cast his eyes on each person at the table.

Sammy asked the question. "Are you God?"

He laughed. "Heavens no, young lady. My name is William Saunders and I am a homeless veteran. I think it is probably my eyes that prompt people to ask that. Of course, when I was younger with dark hair and a dark beard, I was asked if I was Jesus. I did play Him one time when I was in the army. There was a small theater in the town next to the base and I saw an ad looking for actors for a brand new play. No other information was given, but I went to the tryout and won the coveted role of our Lord. After I got out of the military, I grew my hair long and I've been wearing this beard for nearly fifty years."

"Okay, William, or may we call you Bill? What brought you here to our table?" Rick asked.

"Bill is fine, Rick. Actually, a couple of weeks ago, I was ready to move on and head even further south, perhaps Florida, when a young girl approached me. Of course, you all know Hannah by either sight, or by a letter, or phone call you may have received from her. She told me she was an angel and that God had a very important assignment for me. She told me to remain where I was until I was contacted again. I was not to eat, nor drink, nor bathe during this time of waiting. She told me that my reward would be the most marvelous gift a person could receive. So I do apologize for my unwashed state. It is pretty hard to say no to God. Of course, you all know that too." He chuckled and when he smiled, his teeth were white instead of yellow as they had been when he arrived.

There was a very perceptible diminishing of his scent and before their eyes, his clothes began to look cleaner. The dirt on his hands and face was disappearing and his matted beard was becoming whiter and fuller, along with the hair on his head, and his eyebrows as well. The creases and crinkles around his eyes reduced and although he was only in his mid-to-late sixties, he looked at least ten years younger than he did just minutes ago.

When Bill saw everyone staring at him and whispering among themselves, he also noticed some of the physical changes they were seeing. His breathing improved and when he took a deep breath, he was able to enjoy the many different scents wafting through a restaurant. That was such a pleasant experience, one that he hadn't had in a great length of time, years actually. He also felt his insides relaxing. He had been very tight for many years, but now all the aches and pains he experienced from time to time seemed to be abating. He shrugged his shoulders and rotated his neck around in a circle and he was free of pain in his upper body. Bill thought that his legs felt stronger, but he wouldn't be sure until he stood up and walked around.

Patrons in the restaurant also noticed the air clearing and the changes in Bill. More than one diner believed they were in the presence of God, but they were only in the presence of God's ongoing work. However, God, in the disguise of a waiter, walked through the restaurant, causing everyone to go back to their meals and their conversations, paying more attention to their table companions than the table where the eight people sat. He disappeared moments later.

The food came, and everyone prayed and then ate with gusto. They enjoyed a goodly amount of wine and beer. The waitress came to the table carrying a bottle of champagne. "The owner would like you to share this bottle before you leave. I'll bring glasses shortly. Also, there will be no check and he's giving me a double tip and a bonus. Don't ask me why, but I'll take it." She smiled and uncorked the bottle.

After they finished, Bill said, "I don't have a place to stay. Could someone suggest somewhere I might get a room, and I also will need some money to pay for my lodging and to either wash my clothes or purchase a new outfit."

Aaron Pammer replied. "Bill, you can stay with me. There are two queen size beds in my room, and now I know why they insisted I take that room, at a reduced rate. I have some clothes that will probably fit you pretty well." He smiled.

After The Gathering, Bill and Aaron spoke often on the phone and last July, on the first anniversary of their meeting, Bill came to Hellertown for a two week visit, enjoying the company of his friend, and finally meeting Lynette, Aaron's wife. Now his friend was gone and the hunters had to complete this mission, hopefully with no further loss of human life.

17

Hearing noise, Mandy and Bill cautiously climbed the steps into a sixteen inch gun loading area, slowly looking around, firing their squirt guns at about a dozen spirits, eradicating them as fast as they could pull the triggers.

Then, Mandy screamed and stopped shooting as a ghost stood in front of her, a look of sadness on its face; it was Maura. Mandy mentally recounted what happened to her friend on Masonboro Island two years ago.

18

A ghost had managed to possess Maura, and the spirit forced her to grab her husband's nine millimeter pistol with a full magazine. Jason never went away without his weapon, but he also hoped to God he would never have to use it.

She raced toward Jason first and he never saw her coming. She raised the pistol and fired three rounds point blank into the back of his head. His face disintegrated as blood, bone and flesh spread out catching Darrell and Mandy totally by surprise.

Mandy recalled that she was fast, but not fast enough as a bullet tore into her shoulder, spinning her around, taking her to the ground, screaming in pain. She couldn't believe what was happening and she was certain she was going to die as Maura leveled the gun at her again. She saw Maura's red eyes and when her mouth opened, spittle spewed out. Just before she fired, Darrell leapt at her, probably hoping to disarm her, but Maura caught his movement and turned the weapon on him, catching him with four rounds. One tore into his face, one took his left hand clean off at the wrist. Two hit him in the chest and he fell like a sack of garbage. He was dead. She put a fresh clip into the gun.

Maura turned back to Mandy, who was pleading for her life. Mandy saw a glimmer of something human again. That moment was all Maura needed to say "Goodbye, Mandy." She turned the weapon on herself, pulling the trigger and not letting go as she danced with the impact of each bullet.

The evil spirit inside Maura exited her body and Mandy took him out with six shots of holy water.

19

Now, two years later on the great battleship, Mandy saw tears in the eyes of her friend's spirit and she heard her speak. "Mandy, I am so sorry for what I tried to do to you, but I was not myself. I want to be with Jason again, and I hope if I see him, he will forgive me. Please send me to him, Mandy. I have been wandering in the darkness of Purgatory and I want to be in the light again."

Maura opened her arms and lifted them above her head. Mandy fired two holy water bullets into her friend and watched her dissolve. She was happy when she saw Maura's spirit spiral upward and she hoped she and Jason would have a wonderful eternity in God's Kingdom.

20

Bill and Mandy stood mesmerized for a moment, watching Maura head to heaven and that moment of unawareness nearly cost them their lives.

A werewolf appeared from its hiding place inside the breech of one of the big guns, racing toward the two humans who were looking upward. The wolf tried to suppress a growl, but it came out, ruining the stealth of the beast.

Mandy saw it first, and grabbed her bow from off her shoulder, hurriedly getting an arrow ready as the wolf closed to within about eight feet. The magic bow and arrow grew to adult size and she pulled the bowstring back as far as she could and loosed the arrow, nicking the wolf's heart, but not taking it down. The large animal leaped through the air and fell on Mandy, knocking her to the floor, breaking her left arm.

Mandy screamed as the wolf bit her right ear, tearing it completely off and its claws were digging into numerous spots in the woman's body. The pain was unbearable, but Mandy fought it off as best as she could.

Bill had loaded an arrow in his bow and got behind the wolf, shooting the arrow into its back, hoping to hit its heart. He missed, enraging the creature. The animal got off of Mandy and turned to him, slashing out at the man's stomach, tearing flesh, but not deep enough to cause more than superficial damage. Bill dropped his bow and grabbed an arrow, poking the animal, trying to find its heart, but to no avail.

The creature wrapped its huge front legs around Bill and lifted him into the air, squeezing the breath out of his lungs. A couple of moments before his air would expire, the animal groaned. Mandy was able to shoot an arrow, using her feet and her right arm, God's grace allowing it to fly straight and true into the wolf's heart, dropping it like a stone, saving Bill's life.

The two laughed like hyenas after being that close to death and they would form a bond that would last until Bill would pass away twenty-two years from now.

21

After clearing every space inside the great ship, Clay, Bernie, Sam, and Sammy headed back to the main deck and fanned out on both sides of the gun turrets, working their way to the front of the ship.

They put down a large number of ghosts on the way, and when they arrived at the long front end of the ship, they joined forces again.

Clay and Kyle had just completed a sweep of the bridge area where they were able to get a three hundred and sixty degree view of the surroundings away from the ship.

"Damn, look at all those people looking over here, Clay," Kyle said.

Clay had binoculars around his neck, so he scanned the faces on the Riverwalk and spotted his wife, Lynn. He saw the fear and trepidation in her face and eyes and he wanted to try to get her attention to show her he was okay, but it was impossible at this distance. "My wife is over there, watching what is going on here, but I wonder what they can see."

Kyle took the binoculars and did his own scan. "It looks like they can see what's happening, but there is very little expression on any of their faces. I'm guessing our Heavenly friends put up some kind of invisibility shield. I imagine they can see the ship, and us; but not the ghosts, witches and werewolves."

"The witches aren't on board anymore. After the evil ones became dispossessed, they all bailed. I think they walked back, since their powers seemed to be gone. I'm guessing that our prayers really worked, and they are human again. I do wonder if we will ever see them again."

Clay shook his head, after getting his binoculars back. "Don't know, Kyle, but I'm thinking we're going to be called together sometime in the near future."

Kyle simply nodded and the continued checking out the superstructure, never seeing the man in biking clothes, sitting in the captain's chair.

22

Within fifteen minutes, the survivors gathered together near the bow of the ship, hugging one another. They knew there were still a handful or more of werewolves and

161

possibly some ghosts as well, although they thought they checked out every inch of the ship.

Standing side by side, they scanned the ship as far as they could see and it was eerily quiet. Birds were flying near the ship, but the hunters couldn't hear them. They also were unable to hear the traffic on the two nearby bridges. It was both calming and frightening; the calm before the storm possibly.

The hair on Clay's neck bristled, much like it did just before his platoon came into contact with NVA or Viet Cong forces. "They are watching us, guys: I can feel them, but I can't see them. How about any of you? Do you see anything out of the ordinary?"

They slowly walked toward the first triple gun turret, side by side from port to starboard, searching high and low, so many protrusions in front of them, until they were under the barrels of the big guns. They broke off into two groups to traverse the deck on either side of the gun turrets and superstructure until they would once again walk side to side to the bow.

Suddenly, Bernadette screamed, "They're behind us." She turned seeing the remainder of the wolves approaching them at a quick pace. She loosed an arrow and as it was on its way, she reached for a second.

The first arrow hit its mark, downing a howling wolf, enraging the others as the other hunters turned, shooting arrows into the bodies of the beasts.

Kyle again thought it was much like the Alamo, but he did not want to die on a battleship this day, nor any other. He launched an arrow at the largest wolf remaining, hitting it in the right eye. By the time he had a second arrow loaded in the bow and the bowstring pulled back taut, the wolf was in mid-air, ten to fifteen feet from him. He let the arrow fly and it hit the wolf in the heart, dropping it to the

162

deck. It died growling and swiping its paws at the man, tearing off two fingers on Kyle's left hand.

Sam turned and fired an arrow through a werewolf's side, piercing its heart, killing it instantly, hearing Kyle screaming in the background.

The creatures were upon them and it became a fight to the death between man and beast. Most of them were too close to shoot arrows effectively; the wolves began slashing out with their sharp claws, narrowly missing their adversaries.

Susan screamed. A wolf had landed on her good arm and the pain was incredible because the claws on its hind legs were digging deep into her flesh. Bernie managed to get behind the wolf and took it down with an arrow through its back into its heart. The beast fell on Susan, knocking the wind out of her, but other than that she would be okay.

Only a couple of wolves were left, but they fought for all they were worth until they both fell, mortally wounded.

Hy and Kyle pulled the dead wolf off of Susan, and she sat up hugging them both. They all began to sob, but they were all alive.

Aftermath

1

After the triplets were cleansed of the evil spirits, they hugged their sisters and the seven of them fled the ship. They had no powers anymore and were afraid that the ghosts and werewolves on the ship would know they were no longer supernatural and would attack them, as well. Feeling fear was a new experience and they would have to practice humanity before being able to deal with their new lives

They were planning to walk all the way to Southport, but once they were off the island and ready to head down the main road, they saw a limousine parked by the side of the access road, the driver standing outside of the car. He said, "Welcome, ladies. I am your transportation to Southport. You'll find folders on the seats for you. Please read all the information and then you will know what you are going to be doing with your lives."

They got into the limo; there was food and water waiting for them, and they ate everything and quenched their thirst with great relish. Once their physical hunger and thirst were satiated, they opened their folders and began to read.

Inside each folder were new identities, social security cards, bank statements, literature about the business they were going to be operating, and a key to the building. There was also a copy of the King James Bible for each of them with their new names embossed on the front covers.

The driver pulled up in front of a building on Howe Street.

Seven Sisters Salvation would open in three days, giving the sisters time to start their bible reading and figure out exactly what they were going to do to help the lost souls that would step through their door.

2

On the battleship, Kyle and Bill went below to retrieve Aaron's body.

"What happened to him, Bill?" Kyle asked, viewing the mangled body of their friend.

Bill knelt down, working on straightening out Aaron's corpse to make it easier for them to take him to the main deck. "I froze, Kyle," he answered, looking up into his eyes. "The werewolf came at him from above. I saw it and got my bow ready, but I couldn't load an arrow. My hands were shaking. I had never seen anything so terrifying in my life. My hesitation cost Aaron his life and I will never be able to forgive myself." He picked up his friend's left arm, torn out from the shoulder and placed it on Aaron's chest.

Kyle knelt down beside Bill, who was now crying uncontrollably. "Bill, it could have happened to anyone. Those things are so fast and maybe you would not have been able to get a shot at it, anyway."

Sammy had silently come down the ladder and was standing three feet away from the two men and the corpse. "Bill didn't have a shot at it, Kyle. I did, so I put one through its heart. Things have been so hectic, I haven't had a chance to talk to him. His death wasn't your fault, Bill, and you have to continue on with your life. Let's get Aaron's body out of here and we can talk later."

After they moved the body to the main deck, a stretcher and two paramedics were there to take the body to a funeral home where it would be prepared and sent home to Hellertown. The casket would be closed, remains not viewable and his family would be told that Aaron perished in an automobile accident while he was vacationing down here in North Carolina.

Sammy took Bill's arm in hers and they slowly walked to the stern railing where they looked across the river to the shoreline.

"Bill, you may have frozen, but you really did not have a shot at that werewolf. I saw it and quickly loaded an arrow, firing as soon as I pulled the bowstring all the way back. I think if I would have hesitated one second, you would also be dead. It was really hard losing Aaron but I didn't want to lose you too." She hugged him.

Through his tears, he replied, "Thanks, Sammy. Everything just happened so fast and I was absolutely certain that I cost Aaron his life. I will still have to sort out what you said and try to visualize those few seconds, probably for a very long time, but because you are so positive that I had no shot, it will make it a little easier for me to move on. I hope we will all keep in touch because there will probably be a lot of PTSD going on from here on in. I hope George doesn't call us again for a long, long time." He took her arm and they walked back to the rest of the group.

Everyone left the ship and those who needed treatment were taken to the nearest hospital. The desk would be told of their injuries, but not how they were really sustained. Those who suffered no physical wounds were able to return to their rooms. Within four days, everybody would be back at their homes, where they would wait patiently for another call from George, if he needed them again.

3

With George's help, Hyram was able to get an appointment that afternoon to be fitted for a new prosthetic arm and he would get it before he and Susan were ready to head home. Because of Divine Intervention, answers for necessary questions were given to Hy through George.

He stuck around the hospital, wanting to see everyone when they were released before they headed back to their 'normal' lives, although their lives would never be normal again after seeing what they saw and doing what they did.

Mandy was the first to be released. Her arm was broken just below the elbow. It was set and a cast put on; she saw Hyram in the lobby and smiled, coming over to him and hugging him tightly. "It's been quite the day, hasn't it, Hy?"

He nodded. "Yes, it has. Your arm must have hurt like hell when a thousand pound werewolf landed on it."

"Yeah, it sure did. Knocked the wind out of me too," she laughed, but her eyes showed no joy. "I still don't know how I managed to get the shot off that killed it before it killed Bill. That will be my reward for the pain I went through. Our adventure here today has given me an idea for a book. I think if I write one, Darrell will be smiling down on me from his heavenly perch."

"Yes, I think he will, Mandy." He hugged her again. "Have a great life and please keep in touch. If you ever get to Bethlehem, let me know and I'll buy you dinner.

"Thanks, Hy. Say hello to Susan for me. I need to go home now and get my thoughts back in order and get back to work." She kissed him on the cheek and left the hospital to go to a waiting car.

He was sitting in a chair, reading a magazine, and drinking a coffee, when Kyle strolled into the lobby, his left hand bandaged. Hyram stood up and greeted the Texan, vigorously shaking his right hand.

"How's the hand, my friend?"

"OK, it hurts some, but I was pretty damn lucky to only lose a couple of fingers."

"Which ones are gone?"

"My little finger and my pointer finger. It will make it easier to flip the bird to people, now." He laughed.

Hyram smiled, knowing Kyle was going to go into the ministry and would likely not be flipping anyone again. "When do you start seminary school?"

"I'm going to wait until the fall session, but I'm going to be preparing a lot over the rest of the summer. Ya think I'll be a good preacher?"

"I think you'll be a great preacher. I've known several over the years, but the ones we have at our church are amazing. I hope they stay with us a long time. They are husband and wife and two of the best preachers I have ever heard."

"Glad to hear it, Hy. Someday I hope to get to Bethlehem and see the Star on the mountain. I hear it's a pretty amazing little city."

"It is, Kyle and I look forward to seeing you."

Kyle looked outside and said, "I think that's my ride. Take care, Hy. I'll see you online."

"Will do, Kyle. You too." They hugged and Kyle walked away, turning to wave one last goodbye."

Fifteen minutes later, Susan was brought into the lobby in a wheelchair and Hyram had a look of concern on his face. She smiled and shook her head, so he figured she was okay, She was wheeled out to the waiting car. They hopped in and headed back to Wrightsville Beach.

168

4

The uninjured hunters left the ship and were met by a waiting car. They all decided they were ravenous and needed some alcohol, so Clay told the driver to take them to the Front Street Brewery. Then he punched in Lynn's cell number and waited for her to answer.

Less than a half hour later, they were seated at a large table on the second floor. Most of them could hardly believe it was only 12:47, thinking they had been on the ship battling for the better part of the late morning until at least late afternoon. Time flies when you're having fun, some thought.

Lynn raced into the restaurant and saw Clay seated at a table upstairs. She hurried up the steps, hugged and kissed him and then said, "You crazy, old idiot. How could you get yourself involved in what happened on the battleship? You could have gotten your fat ass killed and then what would I do?"

Although shocked by her outburst, the table erupted in laughter that lasted for a long time and caught the attention of a number of people in the place.

When the laughter died down, he said, "I love you too, Honey."

That simple statement brought on another laughing jag. Lynn couldn't help laughing either.

"Folks, this is my wife, Lynn." He rattled off everyone's name for her and then she sat down. "I'm so glad you are all okay, even though Clay didn't tell me what happened today, but I know him and his FBI antennae have been working overtime since breakfast yesterday. I guess someday I'll find out what happened, but all I know is that from my vantage point all I could see were you guys and gals running around with squirt guns, water bottles and toy bows and arrows. Oh, I noticed that everybody was wearing glasses, too. If anyone is willing to tell me what occurred, I'll gladly listen."

The friends looked at one another and after Samantha told what she recalled, each one took a turn. They all stopped talking when the waitress took their food and drink orders, and then continued the conversation continued until the server returned to the table with their orders.

A couple of hours later they all left to head back to their hotels to finish the week, or head home.

5

Back on the ship, the Holy trio and Satan faced each other in their true forms. God spun a web of invisibility around the ship so curiosity seekers could not see them.

Satan said, "Well, you guys beat me again, but you know there are going to be many more battles between us and the humans we use to fight the battles."

The bright light surrounding God, Hannah and Christian made it difficult for Satan to see, but he changed the focus of his eyes, darkening the Holy light and was able to see God nod. "That is so true, and I know we will lose some battles but we will ultimately win the war."

"Lots of people are turning away from you, so how can you say you will ultimately win? My flock grows steadily every day while yours dwindles. Plus, many of your followers are aging and my minions are from the youth of humanity. I have struck out at the people of earth so many times, causing grief and havoc, and yet your leadership refuses to pass laws to make it harder for my people to keep killing and maiming. I think you will lose in the end."

170

"Some of what you say is true, but unless I pull the plug, this world has a long time to go and I see much repentance on the horizon. Now I think it is time for you to take your dead off this ship so people can enjoy it again."

Satan waved his hands back and forth, disintegrating the werewolves' bodies and cleaning all of the wet spots left by the ghosts he thought would give more of a battle. Then, he disappeared.

God removed the web and gave Christian a hug before He and Hannah disappeared. The boy found his parents, knowing he would meet his Father on earth again.

Wrightsville Beach, North Carolina
July 15th, 2016

1

Laurence Hastings had just returned from the beach. While there, he took a half hour walk, as a beautiful sunrise appeared over the ocean. He tested the water, and read thirty pages of a new novel. He placed his lawn chair along the foundation of the old Inn, and then hung his wet towel on one of the wash lines provided for guests.

Steve Wright was walking across the street after checking his cabin cruiser that was docked on the Intracostal waterway, that many people called the Sound. He saw Laurence and waved to the older man.

"How are you on this fine morning, my friend?" Steve asked.

"Still a bit achy from my fall the other day, but other than that, I am quite splendid. How could one not be splendid spending time at the beach?"

"That is true, Laurence. I can't imagine spending my life anywhere else but the beach. I don't know how many years Mary and I will continue to run this place, but Paul and Rachel might take it over. I'm sure Molly will help them out."

"Molly is a fine young lady, Steve. You must be so proud of her. Her modeling career will probably really take off once she finishes with school."

Steve lifted the lids of the trash cans, to see if they were getting full. "Yes, she is really doing great. I support almost everything my family does. So, how badly does your body hurt today?"

My hands will be okay eventually. My knees took the beating, and the soreness will probably last awhile. It's tough getting older. I remember an older friend, I think he was about ninety-two at the time. He fell backwards over one of those concrete car stops in parking lots. He landed on his back, and after a few moments, he got up as though nothing happened. He was a bony, old guy, too, so I figured he'd suffer from that fall. This spring, he turned one hundred and he still lives in his house, cuts his grass, and works part time. He is amazing, but he is one ornery old cuss."

Steve laughed. "Sort of an older version of you, isn't he?"

"Sadly, that is true. I thought I would mellow more in my old age, but after teaching for all those years, reading some of the crap that my students wrote, I thought I was a poor professor."

"Hey, I taught for a while, too, you know. Some kids just don't get it, but most of them will wind up okay eventually. Time to get over it, you old bastard." He snickered at his friend.

"Yes, perhaps you are right. Have you seen Hy and Susan since they returned?"

"No, I think they need more time to process what they went through on the battleship. Perhaps we'll see them at cocktail hour."

2

Most of the week's guests were on the front porch for cocktail time. Steve and Mary had their usual seats on the swing, Laurence was sitting on a wicker chair, sipping wine provided by the two young couples from California, Alexia and Martin Hooper, who were sitting on a couple of chairs

173

that were set up on the porch for additional guests, and Tara and Pete Zander, who were lying side by side on the hammock, sleeping. One of the gay women, Louise Chandler, was sitting on a wicker chair next to Laurence and her younger girlfriend, Charlotte Dixon, was sitting on a wicker chair across from them. The born again Christian couple, Hal and Stephanie Ormond, were on the wicker love seat, with their kids, Christiana and Max on their laps. The middle aged musicians, Cara and Barry Wilkenson, were on plastic deck chairs, playing soft music. The young couple from Colorado, George Mills and Rebecca Wotring sat on the porch steps, smoking cigarettes and drinking beer. Elliot and Lizz Davidson had just stepped onto the porch, bearing plates of cheese and crackers and shrimp cocktail along with a six-pack of wine coolers. They pulled chairs over to where everyone was sitting. The mother and daughter from Pittsburgh weren't there because they had to return to home and had left early in the morning.

"Do you think Hyram and Susan, oh, and Sherrl, will come out to join us this evening?" Stephanie asked, looking toward Steve and Mary.

"I don't know, Steph," Mary answered. "Susan sent me a text early this afternoon, telling me they were still really beat from their adventure. Both of them were hurting from their wounds, but their mental injuries were worse. They had been talking all day yesterday and today with the others who fought the paranormal enemy. Most everyone was having problems and were talking with their spouses or other hunters."

Steve added, "Since what they have done was not witnessed by anyone except those on the ship, the media will never hear the story. I'm going to use the Wright rule when they tell us about their adventure." He pointed to the sign behind him: *What Happens On The Porch Stays On The*

Porch. However, if Hy and Susan tell us any different, you may disregard this rule."

3

Conversation turned to other topics, and much food and drink was consumed in a short period of time.

Fred, the squirrel, was perched on one of the railings, accepting treats from whoever wanted to give him some. He was eating from everyone's hands. Suddenly, he stopped eating and looked toward the door chattering like crazy. The guests stared at Fred because they all heard him say, "Here she comes."

Sherrl Wilhide bounded out on the porch. Her hair was now a rainbow of colors. She wore sunglasses with purple frames and red lenses. She had on a pair of LuLaRoe leggings with cats all over them, and a striped top that she purchased from a consultant in Allentown. Her outfit was completed by orange sandals. "Folks, they are coming down in about fifteen minutes," she said, her Arkansas drawl thick as mashed potatoes.

Steve and Mary gave up the porch swing, so Hy and Susan could be seen and heard by everyone. They grabbed two more chairs from the side porch and after getting a plate of cheese and shrimp, and more wine, they settled down in their seats, looking forward to seeing their new friends again.

Sherrl sat cross-legged on the floor beside the swing, and Max hopped off his mom's lap to come and sit with her. They had really bonded together and, unknown to them at the time, Max would come into her life again when he became an adult, and she would be an octogenarian.

Fred was accepting treats by hand again, but when he heard the stairs creak, he chattered again and jumped from his perch, racing over to Sherrl and Max, winding up on Sherrl's leg. He laid down and quietly waited for Hy and Susan to step out on the porch.

4

When the guests saw Hy with his prosthetic arm gone, and Susan's arm in a cast and sling, along with the superficial wounds they bore, almost everyone gasped. What could have happened to these two, some, if not all, thought? They were about to find out.

Hy grabbed a proffered beer and Susan a glass of wine before they sat down.

"Hello folks, Susan said, through a weak smile. "Hy and I want to thank you all for not bugging us the past two days while we were sorting through everything that has happened to us since the werewolf attacks near the end of last year and through January." She looked at Hyram. "Also the vampire attacks of 2010 and the explosion that cost us our limbs. We have just experienced a battle that no human should have to go through. I can tell you that we eliminated thousands of spirits, eleven werewolves and three evil witches were cleansed of their demons, joining their four sisters as humans. God has given them the opportunity to live out their human lives helping others through a business he set them up in.

"The one thing I don't understand is that a werewolf gouged me, yet I haven't felt any strange effects. My wound will eventually heal, and hopefully I will never turn into one of those creatures." She emitted a nervous laugh. "The others who were scratched seemed to be okay, as well."

After a couple of moments of silence, Hyram added. "I got a call from `the seven sisters and they were so apologetic about the harm they caused over the centuries, although four of them tried to do good for many humans and now with God giving them a free pass, they plan on doing a lot more good until their times are up."

They both spent the next hour or so sharing their thoughts about what had occurred on the battleship, until they returned back here to spend some recuperative time. Both felt that they would have a certain amount of PTSD that they would have to carry, but both of them being strong people would probably better help them deal with it every day.

Hal said, "As a born again Christian, it is still really hard for me to believe in these paranormal creatures, and that God would give those self-proclaimed witches the gift of humanity for the remainder of their lives. It just goes against everything I believe in." Stephanie nodded her head in agreement with her husband.

Steve said, "Hal, what about two years ago when a ghost scared the crap out of you down in Wilmington. How did you wrap your head around that one?"

"I still don't know what to make of that, Steve, but even though I saw something that I believe doesn't exist, there must be a logical answer."

"Well, share that story and let's see what conclusions we come to."

"Fair enough. Two years ago I was on the Riverwalk, heading back to the car after an unsuccessful fishing excursion. Two people were sitting on a bench talking to each other. I was pretty sure the man was blind because he wasn't looking directly at her. He seemed not to be talking to her, but listening to something. I had no idea what to think. I heard him then say something about a man named

Cecil Goodwin. Suddenly something, I'm not going to say a ghost, materialized in front of my eyes, and I was startled enough to drop my fishing rod and empty bucket. The bucket bounced once and came to rest at the woman's feet. I regained my composure and asked, "What's going on here?" pointing to the image. "He just appeared out of thin air. The image smiled. It said, 'I'm a freaking ghost, Sonny. Now grab your stuff and get out of here or I'll haunt you forever.' Now, I was a little frightened, so I grabbed my rod and bucket and high tailed it out of there, looking back as I ran. The image drew a finger across his throat. I didn't tell Steph about it because I realized they make movies down there and I figured I could have been drawn into the scene. Once I thought that, I was okay."

"Good story, Hal, but wrong. The man and woman were Rick and Denise Conlen. At that time he still was blind, but he was regaining his sight. What you experienced was a full-fledged encounter with a spirit, so perhaps you have to rethink everything you have ever learned."

Hal's eyes grew wide with that new knowledge, and it was very upsetting to him. Never in his life would he have thought he would see something he didn't believe in, but now, he needed to talk to his pastor when they went home. All he did was nod and hold Steph's hand. She was pretty shook up too, Hal sensed.

Since the topic of religion came up, Louise said, "Charlotte and I have been together for forty years, ever since we met in college. We've gone to a number of churches, but as soon as knowledge of our sexuality filtered through the congregation, many people shunned us, so after a couple of years we just stopped going. We are believers, but it is hard when you can't practice your religion in a church setting. We still hope that we can be accepted, so after having some talks with Hal and Steph while on vacation, we are going to try again. We both miss worshipping with new friends."

Elliot said, "Lizz used to go to church when she was younger, but since she met me, she has stopped. I am an avowed atheist and I could never get a handle on religion. My folks never attended, so I guess I decided not to go either. I believe in the big bang theory of creation, and I have to admit this discussion is frankly not for me, so I think I'm going to head back to the room." He tried to stand up, but he felt as though he was glued to the chair.

Lizz stood up and tried to help him to his feet, and Steve tried as well, but he was unable to stand up and he became afraid. "I think I'm paralyzed. What the hell happened to me?" He looked straight through Hy and Susan, seeing George and Hannah. They pointed to his legs and then folded their hands in prayer.

Elliot closed his eyes and folded his hands, doing something he had never done before. "Lord, I am sorry for not ever believing in you. Please remove this paralysis from my legs and I will serve you until my last breath." As suddenly as his paralysis began, it ended and he could now move his legs. He sighed in relief and said, "I guess I was given the proverbial kick in the ass, wasn't I?" Lizz hugged him, and whispered something in his ear. After they returned home, they both began going to church and within two years, Elliot was a deacon. Their lives became enriched more than they could ever have imagined.

By now everyone was pretty well stunned with the course of events and stories on the porch. It was getting late until Christina asked, "Whatever happened to Walter?"

5

Walter Marchant was busy from the moment the battle began. He had to fight off spirits that didn't want him giving away their positions to the hunters. He'd see a few or a bunch hiding and was able to guide teams of hunters toward them, if there were few, and away if he felt there were too many for two people to take on.

"Samantha and Sam told us that Walter saved their lives when a group of ghosts were bearing down from above. They had few precious seconds to rapid fire into the twenty-two ghosts hurtling down from the ceiling, taking out seven before the twins were able to find more cover under a couple of tables. The ghosts had to go at them two or three at a time and the twins were able to survive the attack, eradicating them all. What Walter had done was pass in front of the brother and sister hunters and then shot upwards toward the horde. He quickly faded away and moved on to help out some more humans." Hyram told this story with great emotion.

"He saved us a couple of times and about five of the others shared their stories of how Walter saved them as well."

Susan said, "After the battle was over, Walter appeared in front of all of us and we thanked him for his help. He asked, 'Am I finally going to get peace and leave this earthbound hell I am in?' We all aimed our squirt guns at him, so we wouldn't know whose holy water bullet was the one to finish him off. He was beginning to seem more human than ghost to us and we figured we'd all be spared the hurt of being the one to send him away. He stood at attention and saluted us as we fired. Many bullets struck him, but none of us knew who fired the fatal shot. He dissolved with a smile and we saw his mist travel upward."

They all had one more full day left before heading back to their homes, so they decided they would try to have a nice going away party the next night.

All the guests were interested in that, but one of the people on the porch was carrying a deep, dark secret.

Cast Of Characters

Pennsylvania

Hyram Lasky-Bethlehem Police Detective
Susan Mitchell-Reporter for Saucon Valley Press
Sherrl Wilhide-Waitress Brass Rail Restaurant, Allentown
Samantha Stewart-Sherrl's friend
Harold Jenkins-Police officer wounded in bombing
Mickey Patterson-Former army medic
Mike McGinnis-BPD, first officer at werewolf attack in
Bethlehem in December, 2016; also first officer to witness
an attack by a vampire in 2010
Nikki Lawson-BPD, Mike's partner
Everett Gardner-Bethlehem coroner killed in attack
Chuck Lawson-Nikki's husband-killed in attack
Lynette Trexler-Chief officer of the werewolf facility
Brandon and JoAnne Pederson-Grandson of Al Pederson
who disappeared aboard the North Carolina in 1944 and
his wife
Lynette Pammer-Aaron Pammer's wife

Carolina Temple Island Inn, Wrightsville Beach

Steve Wright-Co-owner of Carolina Temple Island Inn
Mary Wright-Steve's wife
Paul Gilbert-Steve and Mary's son-in-law
Rachel Wright Gilbert-Steve and Mary's daughter
Molly Gilbert-Steve and Mary's granddaughter
Laurence Hastings-Retired professor and guest of the
Wrights
Seth McGuire-Reporter for the Wrightsville Gazette
Hal and Stephanie Ormond -Born again Christians from
Ohio
Christina and Max-Their children

Fred-A squirrel that hangs out on the porch
Mansur Ahmad-Vacationing surgeon who took video of a witch from a drone
Sameer Rahim-Mansur's friend in the army
Elliott and Lizz Ringgold-Vacationers from Charlotte, N.C.
Martin and Alexia Hooper-Guests from California
Pete and Tara Zander-Guests from California
Louise Chandler and Claudia Dixon-Gay couple
Cara and Barry Wilkenson-Instrumentalists
George Mills and Rebecca Wotring-Guests from Colorado

Southport, N.C.

Walter Marchant-A ghost who passed two years ago
Helen Marchant-His wife, murdered two years ago
Rick Conlen-Once blind attorney who miraculously regained his sight.
Denise Scott Conlen-His wife, paralegal at their firm
Laura Beck-Southport police officer
Mike Solomon-Southport police officer
Lennie Beckham-Walter's army buddy
Stanley and Emma Marchant-Walter's parents
Harlan Sanders-Southport police chief
Elliott Mayotte-Rick's optometrist
Gail Weichert-Walter dated her in high school, but she is actually a witch
Hank Ebert-Walter's army buddy-KIA in Vietnam
Lucy Yates-Walter's neighbor who saw him at home when Helen was killed

The Good Witches

Lucinda Barone-Oldest of the seven at 27 in human years

Eliese Conway-Most beautiful of the seven at 26
Amanda Tarioli-Second youngest of the sisters
Janelle Landon-Youngest witch and she has no eyes
Graeme McDougal-Lucinda's friend, an immortal since 1793-killed in 2015
Riley-Graeme's three-legged dog, also immortal since 1793
Julian Ross-Immortal since 1779
Petra Ross-Julian's wife immortal since 2015

The Evil Witches

Giselle McFadden-Oldest triplet by six minutes
Marta Cullen-Second born triplet
Bella Jansing-Youngest triplet

The Holy Trio

Christian Balliet-God's human son
Mike and Jamie Balliet-Christian's human parents
Peko-Christian's dog, saved though God's power
Hannah-A ten-year old angel
George-God in his earthly disguise

The Werewolves

Adam-Human clone of werewolves now known as Jeffery Grandar
Eve-Human clone of werewolves now known as Vicky Marsett
Jamal Washington-Teenage boy scratched by a werewolf gaining special powers now known as Malcolm Clair
Dr. Willis Little-Vicky's obstetrician
Serena Marshall-Little's nurse

Delroy Addison-Saw the fire at Dr. Little's office and followed the van

The Hunters

Aaron Pammer-Mack Truck retiree from Hellertown, Pa.
Kyle Quinlan-Paralyzed veteran from San Antonio, Texas
Samuel and Samantha Staunton-21 year old fraternal twins from Bar Harbor, Maine.
Steven and Stella Staunton-Sam and Sammy's parents killed when the twins were ten
Bernadette Owen-Leper type malady from San Diego, California
Loretta Owen-Bernie's mother a former prostitute
Dr. Riegger-Loretta's obstetrician
Gene Ramsey-Bernadette's stepfather
Christopher Columbus-Discoverer of America
Cecil Goodwin-Boilerman on the North Carolina during WWII; passed away in '61 after seeing ghosts on his ship
Clay Reppert-FBI agent and Vietnam veteran
Lynn Reppert-Clay's wife
Linde Harmon-Satan's human name
Mandy Fairchild-Fought spirits on Masonboro Island

Others

Mary Jane Thompson-Wilmington police officer
Marcia Logan-Actress friend of Lynn
Kay LaMotte-Bartender at Front Street Brewery
Drew LaMotte-Sailor or board the North Carolina, Kay's husband
Tank Lincoln-Sailor on North Carolina

Maura Wilson-Camper on Masonboro Island possessed by evil spirit and killed herself

About The Author

Larry Deibert has written nine previous books: *Combat Boots dainty feet-Finding Love In Vietnam, The Christmas City Vampire, Werewolves In The Christmas City, The Other Side Of The Ridge-Gettysburg, June 27th 2013 to July 2nd, 1863, Fathoms, From Darkness To Light, Family, The Life Of Riley, and Santa's Day Jobs.* All of his books are available at Amazon.com and at www.createspace.com

He is a Vietnam veteran and was the first president of the Lehigh Northampton Vietnam Veterans Memorial

Larry retired from the U.S. Postal Service in 2008 after working as a letter carrier for over 21 years

He and his wife, Peggy, live in Hellertown, Pa., where he enjoys reading, writing, golf and exercising. He has two grown children, Laura and Matthew.

He is working on several new projects. To find out how to get signed copies from the author, email him at larrydeibert@rcn.com

Made in the USA
Columbia, SC
09 July 2018